THE TANGLED STRING

A Charlie Chan Mystery

John L. Swann

Nicholas K. Burns Publishing
Utica, New York

Nicholas K. Burns Publishing
130 Proctor Boulevard
Utica, New York 13501
www.nkbpublishing.com
nickburns@nkbpublishing.com

First Edition

ISBN 978-0-9755224-7-9 (paperback)
ISBN 978-0-9755224-8-6 (ebook)
Library of Congress Control Number: 2024948089

The following is a work of fiction inspired by the characters created by Earl Derr Biggers. Any resemblance to actual events or persons, living or dead, is entirely coincidental. The book's primary setting is the very real Hotel Statler of nineteen-thirties Boston, although many of its descriptive details were constructed in the author's imagination.

Cover Art by Sarah Marris-Swann
Book Design by Lynne M. Browne

Praise for John L. Swann's first
Charlie Chan Mystery
Death, I Said

"We finally have one! A Charlie Chan Pastiche true to Earl Derr Biggers original novels. John L. Swann has picked up the pen to write a solid novella that remains strictly aligned with Biggers' storyline.

"Exciting news for mystery buffs, who've longed for someone to dare follow up a true Charlie Chan novel, a new mystery to *carry on* with author Biggers' storyline. We have it now in ***Death, I Said: A Charlie Chan Mystery*** by John L. Swann."

Lou Armagno, www.thepostmanonholiday.com, Editor of
The Wisdom Within Earl Derr Biggers' Charlie Chan:
The Original Aphorisms Inside the Charlie Chan Canon

"A thoroughly entertaining story that has the flavor of the original novels, tinged with the spirit of the Warner Oland and Sydney Toler movies. As I read this I personally felt like I was revisiting old friends and happy memories.

"So I'm happy to report that I felt I was reading an authentic Charlie Chan novel. The bottom line, I recommend ***Death, I Said*** by John L. Swann with two thumbs up!

Drew R. Thomas
Worlds-Best-Detective-Crime-and-Murder-Mystery-Books.com

For my wife, Patricia, and our three daughters,
Martha, Sarah and Olivia,
with thanks for their support and
encouraging words.
Their many successful creative endeavors
are an inspiration.

CONTENTS

PREFACE

In *The Tangled String*, the sequel to 2023's *Death, I Said*, I have continued to imagine what Earl Derr Biggers would have done with his creation had death not interrupted the author's original Charlie Chan series. Published in book form from 1925 to 1933 after serialization in *The Saturday Evening Post*, the six novels are not as well remembered as the dozens of Chan movies, but Biggers portrayed a more complex character than Hollywood's beloved-by-some-scorned-by-others version.

Biggers himself described his creation as an attempt to offer a positive counter to the villainous Fu Manchu stereotype prevalent in early twentieth-century fiction and film. His blend of mystery, humor, romance and far-flung settings was also a Midwestern author's good-faith attempt to portray a Chinese-born American citizen living in pre-statehood Hawaii as a heroic figure, triumphing over racist attitudes and low expectations from White police and criminals alike. Thus Biggers created a unique and internationally popular fictional character, one who applied ancient wisdom, scientific detection methods and a keen wit to solve seemingly insoluble cases.

To mark the centennial of Charlie's first appearance in print in 1925, this new series is intended to entertain longtime Chan fans and, perhaps, introduce some twenty-first-century readers to the enduringly popular character created by Earl Derr Biggers. Hollywood may someday revive the Chan of the films, but since Biggers left no draft, no outline, nothing other than his intention to write "another Chan," we will never have another book in his unique voice. I hope that this new series represents both a humble tribute to the author and a respectful likeness of his original creation.

As the detective himself might put it: "Better a broken bit of old jade than a whole piece of new pottery."

ACKNOWLEDGEMENTS

My thanks to all those who continue to encourage these fledgling literary efforts, especially my spouse and three daughters to whom this book is dedicated. The cover owes its striking appearance to my daughter Sarah Marris-Swann, the artist; and to long-time colleague and friend Lynne Browne, the designer. My brother Bruce Swann read early drafts and provided thoughtful feedback, and publisher Nick Burns continues to apply his unique book editing and marketing expertise to our collaboration, for which I am grateful. Above all, I join with generations of countless fans indebted to author Earl Derr Biggers and Chinese-Hawaiian detective Chang Apana, whose remarkable career provided the inspiration for the creation of Charlie Chan.

CHAPTER I

A CITY UNTO ITSELF

The elevator arrived in the lobby with a muffled bang.

Startled hotel guests passing through the lobby turned toward the sound as a few unsteady passengers emerged from the ornate cage-like car. The uniformed elevator operator ignored the rough landing; he was used to it.

"Watch your step, folks. Have a good night."

An occasionally noisy elevator was surely the most undignified feature of this grand lobby. First-time visitors were usually impressed by the coffered ceiling, supported by ornate limestone columns, the sweeping staircase to the mezzanine, dark walnut walls and brass trimmings; the grand piano tucked into a corner and a general atmosphere of comfort and style.

This hostelry was not the oldest in Boston, not the most expensive—but it perfectly combined charm, character and practicality. Guests generally thought it sufficiently comfortable, despite its tendency toward the ornate, and many patrons returned more than once.

Emmet Gilbert, the elevator operator, left the car door open and looked around the lobby for potential passengers. Seeing none, he lit a cigarette and walked to the reception desk for a chat with the manager. It was late in the evening, and few, if any, patrons would arrive now.

"Evening, *Mister* Krednish."

"Emmet." The manager acknowledged the younger man's sarcastic familiarity with a nod.

"Where's McGee?" Gilbert referred to the clerk he had not seen at the hotel for a few days.

"Absent. Again." Krednish replied with a frown. "I plan to have a little chat with him about these all-too-frequent absences, as well as punctuality."

"Speaking of chatting, I'm glad you're here—I've been meaning to come see you." Gilbert paused, exhaling smoke sideways. "Not my place to ask, but—"

"No, I have no new information about the scheduling of the elevator repair." Krednish, a tall, spare figure in a dark suit, had not looked up during the exchange. His attention was focused on an array of ledgers and registries spread across the top of the desk.

The elevator operator persisted.

"As I said, I know it's not my job to fix the thing, just to take it up and down. And I'm used to it. But people are talking, the word's getting around. It can't be good for business." Gilbert's tone was pointed, if not quite insolent, and it irritated the manager.

"The business of this hotel is in good hands, and it doesn't concern a junior member of the staff whose only duty is to—how did you put it?—'take it up and down.' " Krednish had been captain of his college debate team, and he now considered the matter closed.

Leaning over the desk, Emmet Gilbert crushed the half-smoked cigarette in the manager's ashtray and walked toward the open elevator without replying. He had Krednish's number and treated him accordingly.

Not my problem, he thought, *if Krednish and the owners want this creaky old thing to bang up a few paying customers every so often.*

Krednish, who correctly read the silence as disrespect, resented the intrusion on his domain. And the addition to his ashtray. He addressed the retreating underling in a rising voice.

"I hardly think this establishment's clientele will think twice about a bumpy elevator ride—we're not the Ritz, after all!"

The manager's raised voice had fairly echoed in the vast lobby, and he punctuated "the Ritz" by slamming open yet another ledger, focusing his eyes on its columns of words and numbers.

Silence reigned, but only for a few seconds.

"Excuse this interruption—"

Startled, Krednish snapped to attention. A middle-aged man stood a few feet from the desk. *How long has he been within the sound of my voice?* the manager wondered.

"I beg your pardon; may I help you?"

"Yes, please. I have reserved suite of rooms for, perhaps, one dozen persons—"

"One dozen?" An attempt to conceal his astonishment failed. "And what do you mean by 'perhaps'?"

The manager's reaction was prompted in part by the stout man's unusual appearance, "unusual" for Boston in the late nineteen-thirties, and unprecedented in the Statler lobby. A dark-blue three-piece suit and dark Fedora stood in stark contrast to his foreign visage.

Krednish's experience of men from far-off lands was limited to the nearby laundry. Never had he ventured into the South Boston district that was, to his New England eyes, another world entirely.

"One dozen, perhaps," his visitor repeated, smiling slightly. "The imprecise figure was mentioned in letter

I sent to this establishment one month ago. Reply from your hotel"—he pulled a folded sheet of paper from an inner pocket—"agreed to accommodations for approximate number of guests in party, exact number to be made final upon arrival."

He handed the letter to the manager, whose demeanor was transformed.

"Oh, I see; of course! I had no idea, that is—I mean—"

"Reserved suite of rooms is ready to occupy? The hour is late."

"Of course, of course!"

Krednish handed the letter back and pressed a button to summon a bellboy. Seizing the registry he had lately opened with a bang, he turned it around to face the hotel's new guest and handed him a pen. The manager knew from scanning the letter what name would be entered, but he couldn't help watching as "Charlie Chan, Honolulu" was inscribed in Spencerian script.

"And the other members of your party?" Krednish inquired, repositioning the registry.

"Delayed until tomorrow," Charlie Chan said promptly. "For tonight, I will occupy hotel suite alone. Also," he turned to the arriving bellboy, "only this suitcase. Trunk will arrive tomorrow, I hope."

Oddly, Krednish beamed with the hearty insincerity of a carnival barker.

"Naturally. We will await the other members of your party and your luggage, and I hope your stay—and theirs— will be pleasant indeed! And may I commend you on your choice of accommodation? Of all the hotels in the city, we are best suited to make you and yours very, very welcome."

"Thank you so much," Chan replied blandly. "This hotel was recommended by Boston friends of longstanding."

A hint of a smile came and went as he turned to follow the bellboy to Emmet's waiting elevator.

"Also, the Ritz was full."

The manager took in the remark and gazed intently at the back of his unusual guest as the elevator doors closed.

A decade old and still Boston's tallest building, the 14-floor Hotel Statler was a city unto itself. Capable of accommodating more than 1,300 guests, it was much more than a home away from home for weary travelers, many of them salesmen.

Each guest room was innovatively luxurious, with a private bath, radio and telephone. For the hungry and disheveled, the hotel boasted an excellent restaurant and guest services such as laundry, barber and shoe-shine shop. Those who fell ill during their stay could seek treatment in the hotel's own medical facility, a complete hospital with operating room, equipped to treat all complaints. A hotel ballroom accommodated large gatherings, formal and informal—including weddings.

Staid and elegant on the outside, the Statler inside alternated between brisk comings-and-goings and occasional late-night lulls that allowed the staff to catch its collective breath. During peak activity, the ornate lobby's human stream and conversational murmur was like a stock exchange trading floor's quieter cousin.

By the thousands they came and went: commercial travelers, businessmen, tourists; but also the well-to-do and famous, presidents and potentates—even the Hollywood elite. Not everyone of means aspired to the dubious privilege of paying fifteen dollars a night at the Ritz-Carlton when they could lodge quite comfortably at the Statler for no more than five.

Charlie Chan, whose periodic brushes with fame added nothing to his modest salary, had acquiesced when his Boston hosts insisted on accommodating the traveling family at the Statler. On this occasion, he was glad to be guided by daughter Rose. She had lived on the mainland for several years and, of course, her life choices had created the necessity of bringing the family to America's East Coast.

The Winterslip family, if not exactly "Boston royalty," were certainly eminent and affluent. Charlie had come to know two of them—John Quincy Winterslip and his Aunt Minerva—in Hawaii some years ago, when their cousin Dan Winterslip was murdered. The detective's solution of the case was his first major professional achievement, and others had followed.

Less than a year before arriving in Boston, Chan had visited Rose in San Francisco. There again, he had found success by unraveling a tangled skein of events at the university where Rose was a student worker; and John Quincy, a longtime San Francisco resident, had again offered investigative assistance—as had Rose.

Once the case was resolved, the two "young people" had become engaged. (Chan still thought of them as children, even though Rose was now in her mid-twenties and John Quincy was at least a decade older.) Rose had convinced her mother to forgo an elaborate traditional Chinese-Hawaiian wedding; she was, after all, a child of the twentieth century and thoroughly American.

And, as John Quincy pointed out, there hadn't been a Winterslip wedding in Boston in many years. Such an event would mean so much to his mother and the rest of the older generation. The Winterslip family would be pleased and honored to arrange for the travel and accommodation of the father and mother of the bride and all of her siblings.

For the Reverend William Pettifather, rector of St. George Episcopal Church, the conflict was always one between spiritual matters and temporal concerns. He was a tall, slender man with wisps of graying hair holding out against utter baldness, and his slightly stooped shoulders gave the impression of a pastor who carried the weighty cares of the parish as though they were his own.

In some sense they were, of course; but he tended to set aside criticisms of last week's sermon, "modern hymns" and other fripperies when his truly personal regrets came calling. In either case, he found little relief in prayer. Perhaps, he thought, perusing the day's paper, the Almighty was occupied elsewhere, or maybe this lowly cleric's past sins were unforgivable.

Dismissing these unhelpful and unholy speculations, he turned from the *Evening Transcript* to the week's calendar: tomorrow, a funeral; the next day, luncheon with the Winterslip women; and, later this week, a wedding.

Even in the midst of a funeral, we are in nuptials, he mused.

In any case, this was to be a "hotel wedding," and his ceremonial responsibilities were reduced accordingly. *We have such a lovely church, but young people have new ideas*, he thought. *Ah, well.*

For a spiritual leader, the week ahead was typical in its variety, and lacking in any potential disruption to his placid existence.

How great are thy works, Pettifather reflected, making a sermon-related note to retrieve the full text of that particular psalm. It had special meaning for him, since he attributed his calling and comfortable position to a divine plan.

The "works" had, in fact, worked out quite well as far as he was concerned; did he not serve others in useful ways and provide guidance to those who needed it?

Rector Pettifather was well pleased.

The woman awoke to the same room, again. It was a pleasant space and lacked nothing for her continuing comfort. People came and went, seeing to her needs.

Half asleep still, she tried to recall what day it was. Sunday? Tuesday, perhaps? She had no calendar, no means of determining the day of the week or even the month of the year.

She was in a kind of stasis, though she did not know the word. Nor would she have thought her existence "stagnant," but it was. Days and nights came and went, like the people who saw to her comfort, and very little changed, as far as she could tell—which wasn't very far, in fact.

She arose, dressed and made her way to the sitting room where she spent most of her waking hours. It had no window, but an anonymous artist's winter landscape adorned one wall. She looked at it daily and wondered who had painted it and what place it depicted.

As she had yesterday, and the day before that, she briefly considered where she was, and why. Again, her daily regimen repeated itself as those questioning thoughts went unanswered and faded away.

She sat on the only chair in the room and waited. Breakfast would come soon, as it always did.

The Winterslip sisters, as many in their social circle thought of them, were not siblings; they were sisters-in-law. Miss Minerva Winterslip had never married, although she sometimes regretted that a long-ago chance for romance had come to naught. A petite, birdlike woman who had passed her sixtieth birthday, she possessed a keen intellect, strong opinions and a continuing interest in the doings of family and friends.

Only once had Miss Minerva left Boston for any length of time. Several years ago she had spent weeks visiting what some Bostonians still called the "Sandwich Islands," where she had experienced life in a more vibrant—and violent—way than ever before. She and nephew John Quincy Winterslip, with whom she had shared that Hawaiian adventure, had been frequent correspondents ever since her return to Boston.

Mrs. Grace Winterslip, John Quincy's mother, resembled her sister-in-law in many ways, superficially. Roughly the same age, they appeared to be archetypal New England women of the upper class, whose physical similarities owed something to inherited Puritan characteristics.

But Miss Minerva's sharp-featured inquisitiveness was absent from Mrs. Winterslip's demeanor, which alternated between a dithery absentmindedness and occasional flashes of common sense—like a gray sky pierced by glimpses of sun.

Miss Minerva was practical not only in attitude, but in most of her life choices. Despite the family fortune, she lived alone in a modest apartment—a former carriage house—just down the street from the family's century-old house. She dined out infrequently, preferring simple fare at home and weekly meals at the Winterslip residence, and she had adopted unostentatious fashions over the years that, some said, bordered on the eccentric.

"My dear, *must* you dress like a peasant?" Grace asked her frequently.

In sharp contrast to Miss Minerva's restraint, Mrs.

Winterslip lived boldly and unapologetically. She was, after all, the matriarch of the Winterslip clan, its de facto head since the passing some years ago of John Quincy's father.

The family branch was a small one. Grace's husband and Miss Minerva had only one sibling, a younger sister, Cora, who had left home and, it was said, died under circumstances too painful to relate. Thus, Mrs. Grace Winterslip and Miss Minerva were the last of their generation.

The younger family—distant cousins mostly—had scattered far and wide, but pride of place still counted for something in Boston society. Grace reigned over a Winterslip household, maintaining a domestic staff better suited to times past, and welcomed visiting family members and guests to her table frequently.

Whether alone or dining with a dozen visitors, she enjoyed what the French called the "pleasures of the table" and made sure her guests lacked for nothing.

"Such wasteful extravagance," Miss Minerva often told her.

If their social circle sometimes wondered at Miss Minerva's no-nonsense attire, they were equally bemused by Grace Winterslip's fashion, which bordered on the regal. Morning, afternoon and evening wear, and jewelry so gaudy—rings, necklaces, chokers, etc.—that more than one acquaintance had sniffed that the stones were no more than well-wrought imitations.

When confronted with word of this gossipy revelation, Grace responded in keeping with her personality.

"Fake? Good heavens, how naïve people are, thinking that a Winterslip would resort to subterfuge in a matter of style! My dear, of course the stones are paste! Only a family of means, refinement and good judgment would be so gauche as to display itself otherwise.

"You see, don't you," she once explained illogically, "that only an uncouth *nouveau riche* person would call attention to herself by parading about with a queen's ransom on her bosom and fingers? *Quelle horreur*!

"Naturally, a Winterslip wears the finest faux gems available, allowing people to believe that they are real—and, of course, they appear to be real, almost, so that people think they've made a great discovery in announcing that they are fake.

"Q.E.D., you see."

John Quincy thanked his stars that among the many fine qualities he had inherited from his mother, her unique faculty of reason was absent.

CHAPTER II

AT THE END OF THE CORRIDOR

Molly was irritated, and she made it plain to the person on the other end of the line.

"Yes, McGee. All quiet, and—"

McGee had more to say, much more. The lobby was silent as the reception desk clerk pressed the telephone receiver to her ear firmly, at first; then loosely, as the volume increased.

"McGee! Pipe down and don't worry." The clerk's patience with her co-worker was elastic, not eternal. "I'm just as prepared as you are, and I know a party of this size these days will be a bit of a strain on the staff, but—"

The chattering in the receiver resumed.

Molly's last name was Meek, which she was not. Church, job and Royal Giants baseball were her life's priorities, in that order. A devoted member of Roxbury's St. Mark Congregational Church, she tried to practice what the Reverend Laviscount preached, but living in Boston had not dulled a steely disposition. The easy liquidity of her native Richmond accent, almost a drawl, gulled co-workers and hotel guests when necessary.

Molly Meek was always clad in the dark-blue uniform of the hotel staff, her helpful expression framed by tortoise-shell spectacles, and hair straightened in keeping with the growing popularity of that fashion. She owed the front-desk clerk position to an influential member of the League of Women for Community Service, and hoped to manage a hotel someday—but not this one.

The relative freedom of working nights allowed her to follow the fortunes of the Royal Giants, and from the Playstead to Lincoln Park she rarely missed an afternoon home game. Today, she was fulfilling the end of the day shift in advance of her regular duties.

Charlie Chan had emerged from the elevator and was approaching the reception desk.

"I have to go, McGee. Duty calls. See you later on."

She hung up the phone and offered Chan the professional smile reserved for important guests in good standing.

"Good afternoon! Mr. Chan, I believe?"

"That is so; am currently lodged in third-floor suite," the detective returned. "I am pleased to make acquaintance of capable person in charge of arrival desk, Miss—?"

"Please, call me Molly," she replied. "I understand from Mr. McGee, the member of our staff I was just speaking to, that you're waiting for the rest of your party to arrive? I hope that you've found everything in order so far."

Chan assured her that the suite appeared capable of accommodating his family. "Happy to now confirm party of twelve, including self," he noted. Meek assured him that, depending on the time of their arrival, the travelers could satisfy their likely hunger in the hotel restaurant.

"I expect arrival soon, according to most recent telegram received," Chan said. "Eldest daughter now meeting mother and ten siblings at the large train station."

"Ah, you must mean South Station," she said with a smile. "Yes, it is the busiest in the country, I believe."

This bit of small talk out of the way, the clerk returned to business.

"Perhaps, Mr. Chan, before they all arrive you might share with me their names for the hotel register? That will save time and make their arrival a bit easier."

She had grasped the register and a fountain pen while speaking and waited for Chan to begin.

"Yes, please. First, Mr. and Mrs. Charlie Chan, Honolulu, Hawaii; and all names that follow also reside there." He paused a moment for the scratching of the pen to conclude the first entry.

"All share last name of Chan, of course," he continued, "and these ten are Henry, Conley, Samuel, William, Thomas, Edward, James, Evelyn, Harvey, and youngest of all, Barry."

Chan had recited the names, from oldest to youngest, in a measured way, and Molly Meek wrote rapidly enough to capture every syllable. Only Rose was missing from the family census, since she had arrived earlier and was the guest of Minerva Winterslip.

"Excellent, thank you, Mr. Chan." She set the register aside. "Since you've already taken possession of the suite and have a key, we just need to welcome your family and make them feel at home. Our staff will be happy to help with what will surely be a good deal of luggage?"

"Doubtless the baggage will fill this lobby," Chan said with a broad smile. "This is first journey of its kind for family, and lack of experience with changeable Boston weather has very likely contributed to the packing of many garments—some useful, others not so much."

"Perhaps I can suggest—"

Molly Meek's suggestion was abandoned as she looked to the main entrance, where a small parade of Chan family members was making its way into the hotel.

Spying their father, the younger Chans scurried across the lobby, overwhelming the detective with hugs and cries of greeting. The older siblings and their mother followed close behind in more dignified fashion.

"Hi, Dad!" Rose greeted her father with her customary exuberance. "The train was on time, and we were able to get everyone in three taxicabs—all the luggage, too."

"Grateful for daughter's successful retrieval of family and cargo—hope no one had to ride in trunk of taxi?"

Rose laughed, gave her father a peck on the cheek, and turned her attention to quarreling siblings. She had often played peacemaker when they were younger, and they still heeded her, mostly.

Chan's wife, Chan Chun Shee, greeted him in their native tongue; she was clad as always in traditional attire, preferring to leave American ways to her husband and their children. The Chan offspring honored their father, head of the family, but recognized that their long-suffering mother ruled the household.

Mrs. Chan clapped her hands to gain their attention, and the group—assisted by three bellboys who appeared as if by magic—made its way toward the elevator, an object of great interest to the younger Chans.

"Dad—will we all fit?" This from Evelyn, Chan's younger daughter, whose many concerns often prompted teasing from her brothers.

"Silly!" said Harvey. "If we don't all fit, we'll make two trips."

"Maybe we could take the stairs?" Evelyn replied nervously.

"Please," their father interjected. "Your parent has two suggestions. Henry, please remain here with your mother and all brothers and sisters excepting Evelyn and Barry. Await next available transport to upper floor or take stairs."

Henry, serious and dapper in a three-piece business suit, nodded and lit a cigarette.

"Second," Chan looked down at Evelyn and Barry, "let us leave operational details to expert and observe sacred American custom of silence during elevator ride."

He shooed the two Chans into the elevator car, where a detachment of bellboys had already assembled stacks of luggage, leaving just enough room for the three passengers and operator.

"Third floor, please," Chan said.

"What's sacred about the elevator?" whispered Barry to his sister, who hissed in his ear: "Shhh! He was kidding, goofus."

Thanks to the Statler's expansive definition of the term "suite," the entire Chan party was accommodated. In addition to the requisite number of beds, supplemental cots—greeted with enthusiasm by the younger children—provided sleeping capacity for the expansive family. The initial flurry of unpacking and claiming storage and sleeping territory was still in progress when there was a knock at the door.

Chan responded to find a middle-aged man of less than average height clad in a rumpled suit, battered hat in his left hand, the other extended in greeting.

"Mr. Chan? The manager told me you were here with your family, and I wanted to pay my respects as a brother officer.

"I'm Watkins, house detective," the little man continued. He didn't always call on visiting police and detectives who stayed at the hotel, but Chan's reputation in California had made its way east.

Brody Watkins was eager to meet a well-known detective, one who would be making the hotel his home for several days. Maintaining cordial relations was a specialty for the gray-haired house detective who had spent twenty years on the Boston police force and almost twenty in hotel work.

"Pleased to make acquaintance of fellow detective," Chan replied courteously, shaking the proffered hand. "I trust this visit is purely social—no official or professional reason?"

"No, no—not at all, not at all." Watkins clutched the brim of his battered trilby with both hands. What does one say to a famous police detective? "Just a chance for me to extend the courtesy of the hotel to you and yours, and to let you know if there's anything I can do during your stay—"

He paused, at a loss for words. Chan delivered a nod that was almost a bow.

"Thank you for extension of hospitality. I regret that family chaos"—the clamor in the suite continued— "prevents me from inviting you to enter for conversation. Perhaps we will meet again, elsewhere in hotel, during our stay here?"

Relieved at receiving a gracious exit cue, Watkins smiled awkwardly.

"That'd be a fine thing, thanks very much. I look forward to seeing you—happy to buy you a cup of coffee, or maybe . . . tea." He belatedly recalled that the Chinese preferred the latter.

Chan replied in the affirmative, smiled, nodded again, and closed the door. He thought it odd, this courtesy call, but perhaps this Watkins was such a man—one of those who did such things, with or without hidden motives.

The hotel detective angled his hat as he had seen Bogart do it in last Saturday night's main feature, and breathed a sigh of relief as he turned from the Chan suite to make his rounds.

Brody Watkins was spry still, even at an age when many of his retired contemporaries wondered why he hadn't joined them. He had never thought of such a thing; after all, he reasoned, his father and grandfather had worked till they died. Retirement was for the very old and infirm.

In addition, pounding a beat in hotel corridors was soft duty compared to his younger days on the force. Every day, and some nights, he arrived at the Statler, hung his trench coat in the lobby cloakroom, offered cheery greetings to co-workers and made his rounds like a good-humored cop on the beat.

His only regret was his darling wife. Now that her health had declined he wished that he could move her from Boston to a warmer place, maybe Florida. He considered their current living situation temporary and hoped to save up enough to finance both a move to a warmer climate, and better medical attention for her.

This damnable Depression, he thought, *keeps a working man down. Pity the poor sods who have no job at all.*
He sighed again, and checked a few more doorknobs to make sure that housekeeping staff were observing the locked-door policy.

Maybe someday things would be different.

Gradually, the weary members of the Chan family retired for the night. Sleep came, even to the younger children, and all was quiet. Even faint noises from the corridor and adjoining rooms eventually diminished and came to an end.

Chan awakened with a start.

The suite was dark, but light under the door to the hallway allowed him to find his way across an obstacle course of beds and cots occupied by slumbering Chans. A quick census revealed one absence, Evelyn; not in her cot, not in the suite's luxurious bathroom.

Charlie Chan was not surprised; he knew his children, and the younger of his two daughters was alternately curious about and fearful of unfamiliar places. She must have gone exploring.

Now wide awake, the detective donned slippers and a dressing gown, exited the suite and scanned the dimly lit hallway in both directions.

No Evelyn.

Always a light sleeper, Chan assumed that he had been awakened by Evelyn's stealthy closing of the door—so she must not have gone far. He hastened past several quiet rooms to the far end of the hallway, and turned the corner.

"Evelyn!" he whispered urgently.

His teen-age daughter, ear to the door of a room at the corridor's end, turned with a start. Seeing her father approaching she put a forefinger to her lips.

Equal parts exasperated and intrigued, Charlie Chan approached his offspring and listened with her, but all was quiet within the room. The corridor was as still as the night.

A few seconds passed, and a parent's patience has limits. Chan tugged at the girl's arm, and she reluctantly moved away from the door.

"Dad—I heard something, and then I saw a lady—"

"Proper time for exploration of hotel will come tomorrow," her father whispered, as they made their way back to the Chan suite. "Be thankful that Mama did not discover your absence and call Boston police."

"But the lady I saw—"

"Please." The detective was firm, but gentle. "Family conversation in dark of night is best adjourned to proper time. I will be happy to discuss your most interesting discoveries at breakfast-time."

The girl yielded to parental authority but indicated thirst. Chan half-filled a tooth-glass from the bathroom and accompanied it with a life lesson.

"Your ancestors would say, 'Yín shuǐ sī yuán.' When you drink the water, remember where it came from."

Concluding the parental negotiations, Chan retraced his steps, shed slippers and robe, and rejoined his wife, who stirred.

"Husband, what calls you from sleep in the night?" Chan Chun Shee murmured sleepily in their native tongue.

"I awoke to find you gone."

"Small mystery, easily solved with glass of water for Evelyn," he returned softly, in English. "I can now report to you that this case is concluded."

CHAPTER III

FACES OF THE LONG DEAD

Beacon Hill's Louisburg Square hadn't changed much in the last hundred years, although parked automobiles had succeeded the previous century's horse-drawn conveyances. Residents of the square's two dozen or so houses, most of them three or four stories tall, represented some of old Boston's Brahmin families. For decades, the Winterslip family had been a presence, holding forth in a stately residence that was even more elegant within than it was without.

The nineteenth-century elite had constructed imposing rows of flat and bowfront Greek revival structures around a small park in which statues of a youthful Christopher Columbus and Aristides the Just now kept watch. Chan's destination, number twelve, was much like its distinguished neighbors on the outside.

Inside, generations of Winterslips had applied wealth and whimsy to their beloved residence. Good taste and the occasional eccentricity of personal choice raised some conservative visitors' eyebrows, but the lady of the house saw no reason to conform to traditional expectations. She treasured the very old and valued the newly acquired.

The overall effect was that of a peculiar museum of American and European furniture, its collection curated by some unorthodox person.

In appearance and demeanor, the butler who admitted guests with an almost unvaryingly grave expression might have been descended from the butlers of Winterslips whose portraits lined the center hall.

"Surely the Almighty broke the mold after your arrival on Earth, Greynebin," Grace Winterslip once told him. "That is, of course, if you were formed from a mold, which I doubt. Probably He, in His infinite wisdom, constructed you a piece at a time, although one sounds vulgar putting it in that particular way."

Greynebin invariably acknowledged the lady of the house and her musings with a muted, "Very good, ma'am," and then tended to his duties.

With the approaching wedding driving the social schedule of the house, Grace Winterslip had instructed Greynebin to prepare for a late-afternoon tea in half of the first-floor double parlor. In turn, the butler had directed staff to make ready a fairly elaborate tea service and accompanying offerings, and to attend Mrs. Winterslip and any early arrivals while he admitted guests.

The room's furnishings were, if not lavish, comfortable enough for the straight-backed descendants of Puritan propriety; and, in keeping with the rest of the house, the parlor's decor teetered between historical hand-me-downs and more recent pieces chosen for comfort rather than thematic elegance.

Mrs. Winterslip had seen to it that Louis XIV and George Hepplewhite enjoyed the company of a Paul Follot settee and its matching lounge armchairs.

"More tea, Reverend Father?"

Rector Pettifather nodded, and Grace Winterslip obliged. High tea in the Winterslip parlor required the fully marshaled talents of the household staff, but the lady of the manse always preferred to serve her guests when holding court, and it was particularly important on this occasion that she butter up the visiting clergy, figuratively and literally.

"And another scone? I do think Matilda has outdone herself, and the extra butter—"

"My word, my word," the clergyman replied, helping himself. "I will scarcely be able to fit into my vestments come Sunday."

"Tut, tut, Rector. You are, if I may be so bold, a fine figure of a man." Grace beamed. "A holy man, of course, although not in any way in a Roman sense."

She reflected momentarily before firing another salvo.

"Strictly high church, doctrinally speaking, but not too high! Yet not at all low church. Your sermons—always scripturally sound, yet quite up to date, not dated."

Another brief pause. The Rector chewed his scone silently.

"Of course dates are important," she went on in the torrent of words and associations familiar to family members and long-tolerant acquaintances. "New Testament occurring in the A.D., Old Testament in B.C. Although always so confusing, it seems to me, the numbers getting smaller as the sequence of events proceeds toward the Zero Year.

"And yet," the patrician brow furrowed, "Zero Year and Year One, one never hears of them—nor are they indicated in the church calendar, are they?"

The Reverend Pettifather swallowed and cleared his throat diplomatically.

"No, indeed, Mrs. Winterslip. Quite possibly an oversight on the part of the early church fathers—"

"If only there had been a few church mothers making notes on parchment or clay tablets or chiseling things into stone, there wouldn't have been any such oversight, I can tell you! Which reminds me, whatever happened after Moses disposed of the stone tablets, you know, after the fuss about the golden calf . . . ”

The Rector was waiting for an opportunity to stem the tide, but the waves continued.

“ . . . and by the by, why did those naughty Israelites pick a calf to worship when a horse or a donkey would have been more apropos, given the circumstances? I mean to say, dear Rector, my point is: How do we even know what the Commandments are since they were all broken into bits? Perhaps we've been observing the wrong set of rules ever since Year Whatever-it-was.”

This feat of theological reasoning would have stumped a lesser man, but the Reverend Pettifather was no ordinary ecclesiastic.

“Dear Mrs. Winterslip,” he replied without hesitation, “You have put into words a scriptural puzzle that has baffled theologians for centuries. Among the laity, only a robust intellect and unique perspective could arrive at the question you posed. Truly remarkable, dear lady, remarkable.”

The Rector, thinking his response both artful and sufficient, sipped tea and silently gave thanks for his verbal gifts.

“You're very free with compliments for a clergyman,” Grace Winterslip replied tartly, “and you haven't answered my question. Indeed, if all the king's horses and all his theologians have been puzzling over the broken tablets all this time—well, either they've put those Humpty Dumpty commandments back together, or Moses jotted them down elsewhere.”

“Beg pardon, ma'am.”

The Rector was saved from further replies by Greynebin's

voice through the doorway.

"Mr. and Mrs. Chan, Miss Chan, and Mr. John Quincy Winterslip," the butler intoned, and departed for other duties. All rose to welcome the newcomers who stood in the center entrance hall; greetings and introductions ensued, and the new arrivals joined the tea-and-crumpets fray.

Ever observant, Charlie Chan lingered briefly in the hall to admire the past few generations of Winterslip portraits; he could see some of John Quincy's facial characteristics in the framed visages, and Miss Minerva's was among the other resemblances he observed.

It struck the detective as curious how the faces of the long dead and all those now living in the Winterslip enclave were much of a piece, as though all of them, past and present, truly belonged at number twelve Louisburg Square. The impression lingered in his mind as he joined the others, and the conversation quickly moved from the general to the specific, the impending wedding ceremony.

The couple had decided on a somewhat traditional American wedding with only a few elements borrowed by the bride from her ancient Chinese heritage, and there were other "adjustments" to tradition that would reflect what would surely be a unique East-meets-West social occasion in Winterslip family history. While Roger Winterslip, John Quincy's cousin and business mentor and senior partner, would serve as best man, the rest of the bride and groom's attendants, by mutual consent of both families, would consist of Rose's ten siblings.

The most visible departure from American tradition, one bound to raise a few Bostonian eyebrows, was the bride-to-be's choice of ceremonial garb. Not for her the typical American white gown, veil and train.

After consulting with her mother, Rose had selected

a Qun Kwa from a shop in Boston's bustling Chinatown. The traditional Chinese wedding gown, splendidly red, was adorned with an elaborately embroidered dragon and phoenix with gold and silver threads. She described it in some detail, and Grace nodded approvingly, no stranger to bucking tradition.

"It sounds lovely, my dear, just lovely," said Grace. If anything, the family matriarch was well pleased with the prospect of a daughter-in-law far removed from hidebound Bostonian conventions. After all, she had enjoyed departing from hallowed traditions, in ways large and small, for much of her life. "And I have something that will, I'm sure, set it off to perfection. A kind of family tradition. But I'll discuss that with you privately when time permits."

"You're very kind—and this is a lovely tea! Very traditional, isn't it?" Rose was eager to please her mother-in-law-to-be. "So elegant."

"Yes, my dear, despite that trouble in the harbor some time ago—silly of those men, dressing up in costumes and throwing away perfectly good tea, and I do believe one of them was a Winterslip—well, many people do prefer coffee now, but I think there's no substitute for this kind of tradition."

Rose hesitated, but her father came to the rescue.

"Great Boston tea tradition and ritual of afternoon consumption of same present interesting parallel to ceremonial customs familiar to Chan family and its ancestors," Charlie Chan remarked. "So appropriate that we prepare to celebrate the joining of two families in this way."

With the arrival of Miss Minerva Winterslip, the conversation fractured. The Winterslip sisters-in-law conducted a lively sidebar, while the Reverend Pettifather went over the essentials of the wedding ceremony with the couple, as the elder Chans listened. Fueled by buttered scones and Earl Grey, Pettifather covered the essentials, answered questions, and peppered his remarks with quips and quotations.

Grace and Minerva, their family colloquy ended, joined the general conversation.

As afternoon marched toward evening, the clock struck the hour and the Rector tendered his thanks for the hospitality (especially the buttered scones) and shook hands all around. Rose's parents, citing the lingering fatigue of travel, begged leave to depart. Miss Minerva took herself off, and the young couple mentioned evening plans.

Soon only the lady of the house and her faithful retainer remained in the Winterslip parlor.

"Family."

Grace Winterslip's single word was directed to the room at large, but since Greynebin was her only audience he felt compelled to reply.

"Indeed, ma'am."

Still speaking mostly to herself, Grace expanded on the theme as only she could.

"Such a great blessing at times, one's kin, but also the source of trial and tribulation, even Sturm and . . . the other thing. Rhymes with rang."

"The word is, I believe, 'Drang,' ma'am."

"That's it. Thank you, Greynebin. You understand about family, don't you? That is, if I may be so bold as to mention it?"

"It's very good of you to ask, ma'am." The butler cleared his throat and continued. "My father is deceased, and I enjoy cordial relations with other members of the family, if I may express it in that manner."

"Cordial, but not especially warm, would you say?

Even though blood is thicker than . . . hmm, most things, I suppose," the lady of the house trailed off.

A silence of several seconds descended on the room.

"Will that be all, ma'am?"

"Yes. Yes, indeed. And thank you, Greynebin," Mrs. Winterslip said kindly.

Inclining his head, the butler gathered the remains of his personal privacy and departed.

"Dad, was there anything about the Rector, the Reverend Pettifather, that seemed, well, unusual to you?"

"Most things about Boston man of cloth seem out of the ordinary to one who has spent life in small tropical island community," Chan smiled. "Something in particular that you noted?"

"Well . . . I'm sure it's nothing, but his quotes from what he called 'the Good Book'—they were wrong."

"Incorrect how, please? Not suited to this occasion?"

"No, no, not that. It's just that—they weren't from the Bible."

Chan's eyebrows raised as he returned his daughter's gaze.

"You know this how, exactly?"

Rose blushed under the parental scrutiny, which echoed long-ago inquisitions in the house on Punchbowl Hill: *What have you learned in school, and how do you know it's true?*

"I'm not a scholar, but I did have a professor at university who taught a class—'Introduction to Comparative Theology'—and he used to put a quote, sometimes from the Bible, sometimes not, at the end of each quiz, to test our biblical knowledge. Most of the students were more religious than I was, and they had studied the Bible in church, but hardly anyone answered his quiz questions right.

"Two of the things the Rector said today—I remember them, because students argued with the professor about them—on 'This too shall pass' and 'God works in mysterious ways' aren't Bible quotations.

"And another thing Reverend Pettifather said," she continued, "'Money is the root of all evil,' I'm sure that's wrong. Not only the words—it actually says that it's the *love* of money that's the root of evil—he said it was the Book of Proverbs, in the Old Testament, and it's really from First Timothy, and that's New Testament."

Chan nodded approvingly.

"Years of mainland education have contributed to keen powers of observation, as well as ability to recall lessons learned." He smiled. "Also you have acquired knowledge of Christian holy writings that adds to childhood instruction in more ancient ancestral teachings."

"It's not that I'm some kind of religious convert," Rose assured him. "It's just that, well, I remembered that the professor said ordinary people sometimes get these things wrong, but the Rector—"

"—not one who should make such errors, after many years of study and preaching to faithful," Chan concluded. "Let us make note of same, you and I, and await further possible instances.

"Maybe only one lapse in mental abilities of spiritual leader, not to be repeated. But nothing should be dismissed in haste. Sometimes the smallest seed grows into a big tree." He grinned. "Something like those words also appears in 'Good Book.'"

Rose laughed.

CHAPTER IV

A SPECIAL DELIVERY

Michael Patrick McCaffrey had come up through the ranks, from walking the beat all the way to detective.

For all of his fifteen years on the force he had been known as "Big Mike," a mostly affectionate nickname that reflected his outsize physical presence and matching personality. He was over six feet in height and solidly built, with an equally large heart and ready wit. Only his intellect and detective prowess were less than large; his professional success owed more to blunt energy and luck than intuition or, least of all, deductive reasoning.

For a detective, he had not had a great many opportunities for detecting. Since donning plainclothes not long ago, his assignments had not yet required anything like ratiocination, but that didn't concern Big Mike. After all, he told anyone who would listen, working crowd security for Father Coughlin and President Roosevelt's visits to the city was a step up from pounding a beat.

Least experienced in the detective division, he boasted no office—just a desk among a dozen in the precinct's common room. It was a busy, dingy area overseen by the captain of detectives, O'Rourke, who frequently peered through his large glass office window. Sometimes he shouted through the open door to summon a suspected idler, a detective who clearly needed an assignment.

Today, it was Big Mike's turn.

"McCaffrey—hey, Big Mike!" O'Rourke raised his voice enough to carry over the hum of activity in the big room.

"Come in here."

Not especially eager for "one of O'Rourke's little chores," as they were known, McCaffrey rose and lumbered into the captain's office. O'Rourke pointed toward a chair, and Big Mike eased his bulk into it. The chair protested briefly; precinct furniture did not always take kindly to an encounter with Big Mike.

"I've got a chore for you," O'Rourke began, looking at a few notes on his desk blotter. "Nothing that will strain you so early in the day"—it was almost noon—"and it shouldn't take long."

"Sure." McCaffrey reserved his reaction. Too much enthusiasm on the job, he had noticed, was lost on the captain.

"It's this way: Some swells want a little package of theirs to go from their bank to the Statler for a big do they're planning," the captain summarized. "And the commission-er has been asked—ever so politely, I'm sure—to provide a reliable man to go along for the ride, just for safety's sake."

He paused for effect.

"Now, then, Michael. You're a reliable man, I'm thinkin'. Aren't you?"

"Sure, and you know it. But what's in the package?"

"Ah—so you *are* a detective after all." O'Rourke grinned. "Well, now! The commissioner either didn't know or wasn't about to tell the likes of me. Not our place to ask such a question, and maybe the less said, the better. Proba-bly some family heirloom or precious trinket that nobody gives a hoot about."

Big Mike nodded. "When and where?"

"I've jotted down the particulars." The captain handed him a note and glanced at his watch. "You don't have a lot of time—the commissioner got the call only this morning. See that you're on time for these folks. 'The Quality' don't like to be kept waiting."

Taking leave of the captain, Big Mike collected his hat and coat. His favorite luncheonette was on the way to the financial district, and if he rushed, he could squeeze in time to satisfy the inner man before tending to O'Rourke's chore.

"I want to have a little talk with you." Grace Winterslip accosted her son as he entered the dining room for a late breakfast. The sideboard displayed food enough for a dozen Winterslips—Greynebin and staff tended to overdo things a bit, John Quincy had noted—even though only mother and son were present this morning.

"Well! And a very good morning to you, too," John Quincy returned, seizing a muffin and seating himself at the table. "I shall endeavor to attend to your every word."

He poured a cup of coffee and offered his mother a refill, which she declined with a wave of her hand before launching into her "talk."

"As your father's son—and mine, too, don't forget!—you have certain responsibilities. Most of them you've neglected, sad to say, running off to San Francisco; such an uncivilized place, I'm sure, and didn't it burn down?"

John Quincy was used to his mother's soliloquies.

"There have been a few improvements since the fire, Mother," he interjected, suppressing a smile. "You're welcome to visit, always. And after we're settled, I'm sure that Rose—"

"That's it," cried the Winterslip matriarch. "Rose! I want to talk to you about your bride-to-be and plans for the wedding."

John Quincy stirred uneasily. What now? Perhaps things had been proceeding too smoothly after all; the combination of his mother's tendencies and the opportunities for extravagance presented by a wedding boggled the mind.

"You've been extremely kind, and Rose—both of us—we're pleased with the arrangements. Do you have something in mind?"

"Of course! That's why I need to talk to you. And there isn't much time to discuss the matter in great detail, but as the groom—and, as I said, the Winterslip heir—you have a certain duty to perform."

"Which is what, exactly?"

"It's quite simple, really," said the woman who could complicate the most elemental matters. "I need you to pick up a package and deliver it. That's all."

"Happy to oblige," John Quincy said cheerfully. "No doubt I'm letting myself in for unnecessary complications, but I am compelled to ask: Why me? Wouldn't Greynebin or one of your many minions do just as well?"

"Silly boy. Don't be impertinent. I have no 'minions,' as you put it. And while Greynebin is quite reliable, this is a task with a certain . . . that is to say, it's a family custom. Before any wedding. And you're the groom, or will be, so it falls to you, this task.

"Not," she continued, "as monumental as a labor of Hercules, but something to be entrusted to the appropriate Winterslip. Not to a servant, even one as trustworthy as Greynebin."

"I'm honored, even overwhelmed—I think." John

Quincy smiled. "I don't suppose you're going to enlighten me as to the contents of this package? Even a general description would be helpful."

"It's not very large," Grace offered. "About this big," she said, her hands describing a rectangle about eight by ten inches. "As to the contents, let's just say that they are important to the family and will play a role of sorts in the wedding."

"You said that I'm to pick up and deliver this item?"

"Yes. From the bank—it's in a safety deposit box—and to the hotel, the Statler, of course."

"Sounds easy enough." John Quincy paused for a sip of coffee; it had grown cold.

"Oh, you'll have no trouble at all, I'm sure. Especially with a policeman."

"A what? Policeman? What on earth for?"

"Only a—what do you call it?—plainclothes officer of some kind, the commissioner said." Grace nodded. "Nothing conspicuous."

"Mother! What am I transporting that requires a police guard?" Suspicions about his mother's "simple" task were apparently justified, John Quincy realized. "And you spoke to the police commissioner—what are you up to?"

"My dear boy—really, it's quite simple—"

I'll bet, her son thought, recalling other maternal plans and plots gone awry.

"—I telephoned Randall–that is the commissioner–to explain plans for the wedding, and I told him that you would be running this little errand for me, and naturally, he's such a good friend of the family, he offered to have a detective accompany you. Purely precautionary, he said."

John Quincy sighed. Providence had apparently deemed it necessary that he be subjected to this particular trial. He knew that when his mother made plans it was useless to oppose them.

"Very well," he said grudgingly. "Your wish is my command, as the genie said. I suppose this little odyssey is scheduled to occur soon?"

"Today. This afternoon. Two o'clock, at our bank. Just ask for Mr. Hallowell, the manager."

"What about my—er—policeman?"

"Randall said that he would have a plainclothes detective meet you in Mr. Hallowell's office," Grace continued. "Your instructions, according to the arrangements communicated to me by Greynebin, are as follows.

"Visit the family's safety deposit box." She handed him a key. "Retrieve the package and proceed without delay to the Statler. Deliver the package into the keeping of the hotelier, Mr. Krednish, for its prompt deposit into the hotel safe."

John Quincy pocketed the key and summarized his itinerary: "Today, two o'clock, Mr. Hallowell's office at the bank. Meet the detective, extract the goods, deliver to Krednish at the Statler."

He saluted his mother good-naturedly. "Will there be anything else, milady?"

"You are incorrigible," Grace Winterslip said affectionately. "However, you take direction very well from a woman, and I predict that your marriage will benefit greatly from that aspect of your character."

The bank was a formidable gray structure, borrowing something from both Greek and Roman architecture, as well as early 20th century American financial hubris. Its builders had seen only growth and expansion in their future, and—to its credit—this institution had weathered economic storms that had swept away many other banks. It had been sheltered, in effect, just as many of its significant depositors had.

The bank's board and most of those depositors had seen nothing wrong with the Hoover administration; they were less sanguine about the current occupant of the White House. Newspaper wits sometimes referred to the institution as the "First National Bank of Brahmins."

John Quincy was well aware of this socio-political backdrop but often felt himself both of his heritage, and somehow beyond it. San Francisco, his home for several years, was no Boston; people out West were not bound by social codes and registries and endless lines of antecedents. Returning to his former world, even for this short interval, aroused conflicting feelings.

Shaking off these reflections, he entered the bank's vast antechamber. Lines of patrons waiting for a turn at a teller's window were dwarfed by lofty ceilings and marble columns, like so many ants streaming slowly toward spilled sugar.

John Quincy went to the manager's office, where he was greeted with the consideration due to a member of the Winterslip family, that is to say, only a few degrees below a royal reception.

"Mr. Winterslip! A great pleasure."

Jefferson Hallowell had a banker's name, and a banker's appearance. A portly frame was clad in a dark, three-piece suit set off by an equally dark necktie; an expression of helpful-yet-conservative concern gazed over and through gold-rimmed eyeglasses; and a modest dark mustache matched his bulbous head of jet-black hair glistening with brilliantine. "Your first visit here in quite some time—how is your mother?"

John Quincy assured him that Grace was well and prospering, and was spared further small-talk by the arrival of a towering figure, hat in hand.

". . . and you must be Detective McCaffrey?" Hallowell smoothly concluded the necessary pleasantries, introducing the two men to each other, and leading the way to the vaulted room.

The manager and Winterslip produced their keys and unlocked one of the many deposit boxes—number 3684—that lined two sides of the vault. Hallowell excused himself, and John Quincy set the steel box on the room's long, rectangular table and opened it.

Lying on a bed of yellowing documents was "the package," wrapped in brown paper and no bigger than a Gideons bible but surprisingly light for its size. The wrapping had been secured with common twine, vertically and horizontally, and a blob of sealing wax obscured the center knot.

"You want that I should carry the item, or just amble along beside you?" McCaffrey asked. "And would you be expecting any particular person or persons who might be interested in it?"

John Quincy grinned. "Amble away, thanks." He deposited the package in a valise brought along for that purpose. "To answer your other question, I have no particular expectation. The lady who assigned me this task thought it would be best to prepare for trouble, just in case."

"Did she, now?" McCaffrey replied noncommittally. "Well, it's the Statler you're going to, so we haven't far to go. And it's a fine day for a walk."

John Quincy's New England youth and years in San Francisco had prepared him for a "fine day" in Boston. An overcast sky with a hint of drizzle, he concluded, was his detective companion's idea of clement weather. This fleeting thought concluded, Winterslip let his mind tackle something more substantial: the contents of the package.

What was so small and valuable that it had to be stored at the bank and accompanied by a burly policeman to ensure its safe transit? His mother, he thought wryly, would no doubt have a convoluted and only partially coherent explanation for these security measures—and their attendant secrecy—when it suited her, and not a moment earlier.

Big Mike McCaffrey kept his own counsel, and his eye out for suspicious characters who might be coveting a package that they couldn't see. Maybe this Winterslip was being followed?

Possibly the item was a stack of thousand-dollar bills squirreled away by this high-hat family? People had strange ideas about money these days, what with banks and stocks and the government all discombobulated. Some people buried their cash in the vegetable garden, and maybe these Beacon Hill folk rented a tin box at the bank to keep some big bills safe for emergencies.

Both men's cogitations were necessarily brief, and the short stroll from bank to hotel passed without incident. Aloysius McGee was on duty at the Statler's front desk, and manager Krednish soon presented himself to receive the expected callers.

"Mr. Winterslip—I've been expecting you." He turned to Big Mike. "And you are—?"

"McCaffrey, detective with the department, assigned to accompany Mr. Winterslip and his . . . package."

"Of course, of course." Krednish nodded, baring his teeth in the semblance of a smile. "I understand that this is—er—a confidential matter. Let's adjourn to my office."

He led the two men down the short hallway near the

elevator, turned a corner and led the way inside the small managerial sanctum. Apart from Krednish's desk and chair, there was room enough for two other chairs; the three men seated themselves. The manager lit a short-stemmed pipe, and John Quincy offered his cigarette case to Big Mike— who declined—before lighting up.

"We're all very much looking forward to your event, I must say." Krednish managed a nearly sincere smile as he brandished a sheet of paper and inserted it into his type-writer. "We have a form for everything," he said apologet-ically. "I'm afraid the hotel's attorneys insist on our doc-umenting any item of value that we hold in trust for our guests."

Puffing away at the malodorous pipe, he attacked the keys for a minute or more to record ordinary but essen-tial information. John Quincy stubbed out his half-smoked cigarette in anticipation and was not kept waiting. The typewriter's bell rang, and Krednish paused, relighting his pipe.

"I've captured the essential information as to names, dates and so on, Mr. Winterslip. Perhaps you could de-scribe the item . . .?" Krednish looked at the valise expec-tantly, and John Quincy withdrew the package, placing it on the desk.

"I would tell you all about it if I could," he said pleas-antly. "But it came into my keeping as you see it here, and my instructions were to deliver it to you. I suggest that we pretend it's Christmas and see what Santa has brought us, so to speak."

The manager nodded and produced a penknife from the center desk drawer. Severing the twine without disturbing the wax seal, he removed two thickness-es of brown paper from the parcel and revealed a slim, gunmetal gray box. Its lid was secured by some internal lock, or so the two men assumed from a small keyhole on the side.

"You have the key?" The two men spoke almost in unison before each realized the answer. Exasperated, John Quincy uttered a single word:

"Mother."

CHAPTER V

"THEY WERE PROFESSIONALS, MR. CHAN"

Emmet Gilbert had a hidden talent.

True, it wasn't the kind of ability that produces fame and fortune; but it satisfied his need to annoy the hotel manager, Krednish, whom he loathed. The reasons for his dislike were a mystery to the rest of the hotel staff, and Gilbert saw no need to reveal them. Whatever they were, the seeds of his hatred sprouted mean-spirited plots—some small, petty; others grand in scale and, as yet, unrealized.

As one of the Statler's two elevator operators, Gilbert had discovered his secret ability quite by accident. Through subtle manipulation of the elevator's controls he could greatly exaggerate its lobby arrival—no mean feat. An occasional, accidental thump was his to command, to increase in substance and volume into a bang—or even something resembling a small clap of thunder.

He combined a mastery of the elevator's quirk with a poltergeist's bag of tricks—locking and unlocking doors at random, and meddling with the efficiencies of order, service and storage that Krednish prized above all things. In these and other diverse ways he satisfied a bitter animosity, plaguing the manager regularly—but always anonymously. His victim never suspected that these diverse and sundry annoyances were the work of an individual.

And Krednish?

The manager did not discriminate; he disdained all the staff, even ones he somewhat tolerated, considering them lower forms of his work-a-day life. Some twist of his personality had soured his view of humanity, especially those specimens he was forced to oversee. Not that Gilbert's random torments went unnoticed by his boss, but Krednish tended to view all such things as further evidence of staff incompetence. Gilbert thought him simply too arrogant to credit even one underling with intentional mischief.

"You see, don't you, that it just won't do?"

The woman opened her eyes quickly, but the room was dark and silent. Only a dream, she thought, but the voice sounded so familiar. She switched on the bedside lamp. *If only I could recall who said those words, then . . . what?* Sitting up in bed, she struggled to arrange her thoughts.

It's a comfortable room, a bit small, but suitable for a single lady such as myself. But am I a single lady? Perhaps I'm married, or widowed—even divorced. How would I know?

The debate was a difficult one; she had to argue both sides of the question, and she wasn't really sure what the question was. Perhaps, she posited, in a brief moment of clarity, there were multiple questions: who, what, where and why.

Who am I? What am I doing in this place? Where is this room? And why have I been put here?

Clarity gave way to mental fog—and the return of doubt.

Greynebin brought "the telephone instrument," as he called it, to Grace Winterslip in the parlor, plugging in the lengthy cord and handing the receiver to the lady of the house.

"Mr. John Quincy is calling, ma'am."

Grasping the phone with both hands, Grace raised her voice to—in her mind—account for the distance; her son was, after all, many city blocks away.

"Ahoy! Ahoy!" The family matriarch hailed John Quincy with gusto.

"Mother?" John Quincy responded. "Have you joined the navy?"

"Well, I've never mastered the art of speaking into a machine," Mrs. Winterslip replied, "but I do recall that Mr. Graham Bell suggested that we greet telephone callers in that manner. Seems perfectly logical when you think about it."

John Quincy sighed.

"Mother, there's no key—"

"Key? Of course there's a key!" Mrs. Winterslip snapped. "You're too young to have a memory lapse. Don't you recall I gave you the lockbox key only a few hours ago?"

"Yes, yes—of course you did, you gave me the key to the safety deposit box," returned John Quincy. "And I'm happy to report that the police detective and I successfully transported it to the hotel."

"Good. Excellent. Well done."

"However, when the manager opened the package—he insisted on doing so—what do you suppose we found?"

"How on earth should I know? Shall we play Twenty Questions?"

"But—how could you *not* know? Really, Mother—"

"My dear boy, let's not make such a pother. I asked you to take the package from bank to hotel, and you have done so. Many thanks. On your wedding day, I may enlighten you—but, to some extent, I am bound by family tradition."

"The hotel needs to know the contents of the box—we removed the wrapping paper—before they formally take charge of it," John Quincy explained, summoning reserves of patience. "It's a question of value, of liability."

"Oh. I see." she paused. "You spoke with the manager, what's-his-name, a Mr. Krednish I believe?"

"Yes, and he was most insistent—"

"I'll call him. On the telephone. I'm sure I can explain things to his satisfaction."

"Shall I put him on? I'm speaking from his office."

Grace Winterslip assented, and her son silently gave thanks, handing the telephone to the manager. McCaffrey crossed and uncrossed his legs impatiently, while John Quincy lit a cigarette and paced in the limited space available.

Krednish pressed the receiver to his ear—he was hard of hearing—and John Quincy enjoyed the series of expressions the manager displayed as he absorbed Grace Winterslip's lengthy "explanation." Apart from facial contortions, Krednish's participation in the conversation was limited.

"Hmm. Yes. Indeed—of course . . . I understand."

Long silence.

"Naturally, Mrs. Winterslip—the hotel . . . quite so. Every precaution."

Puzzled silence.

"And, yes, the ancient Greeks, too. Romans? Just as you say—and thank you. Certainly. I'll tell him. Very well—goodbye."

Returning the telephone to its cradle, Krednish turned a thoughtful face to John Quincy, who had resumed his seat. "Your mother is a—that is, she seems to be—"

"Yes, she is all that, and more," John Quincy said wryly. "I assume that you have been sworn to secrecy?"

"Yes, yes. Mrs. Winterslip explained the need for discretion most . . . thoroughly. And she gave me sufficient information for the hotel's purposes. More than enough."

"No doubt," said John Quincy. "I'm glad we were able to accomplish this—er—secret mission to your satisfaction and the hotel's."

The Winterslip heir and his police companion rose to take their leave.

"Oh, Mr. Winterslip—your mother asked that I tell you—"

"Yes?"

"Not to be such a fussbudget."

Alone in his office, Krednish had wasted little time on the gray metal box. He consulted the desktop calendar and turned to a mirror hanging at eye level behind his desk. He adjusted his necktie, admired the result, and swung open the framed rectangle of reflective glass to reveal a wall-safe. Turning the numbered dial to the correct combination of left-right-left positions, he opened the door and deposited the Winterslip box within.

After closing and locking the safe, he returned the mirror to its functional position and attended to business— there were telephone calls to return, mostly routine replies to vendor inquiries, and a few to staff via the house phone. He relit his pipe, grasped the waiting pile of paperwork from the inbox, and began the wearisome process: reading, reviewing, sorting, stacking, signing, filing.

It was late in the evening, and he had done enough for one day. The manager departed the hotel for home and a well-earned rest.

Charlie Chan was prepared to avoid repeating last

night's escapade. He had double-locked the door, once the family had settled itself, to ensure that Evelyn stayed put. Soon, he joined the rest of his family in the arms of Morpheus.

Waking with the dawn, the vacationing detective was up and dressed when the telephone rang. He barely had time to lift the receiver before an insistent voice sounded.

"Hello? Mr. Chan? This is Mr. Krednish, the manager— we've met, I'm sure you recall—"

The detective acknowledged his identity.

"I'm so sorry to disturb you, Mr. Chan, but could you please come to the lobby at once? There's been an incident, a theft—"

Chan sighed.

"Better, perhaps. that you call on official police since I am here in role of guest," he said softly—family members were still asleep—but firmly. "I have no authority here as visiting policeman."

Krednish was unfazed. His reply streamed through the instrument into Chan's ear in a rush.

"Yes, but—that is, our own detective, Watkins, is here, and he thought—that is, I thought that with your help we can avoid a scandal, and there would be no need for the police, and since this involves the wedding—"

"Ah." Chan was resigned. "I will be with you momentarily."

The lobby was quiet when Chan descended the stairs, greeted by the sight of Krednish pacing and furiously puffing a cigarette behind the front desk.

"Mr. Chan—thank heaven! Please, come with me." He led Charlie Chan toward the elevator into a short hallway, turned to the left, and entered his small office, stubbing out his half-smoked cigarette in a desktop ashtray. Watkins, the hotel detective, was peering into Krednish's open wall safe.

"Detective Watkins was the first person I called when I discovered that the safe was open, and empty," Krednish explained. "I think you've already met?"

"Glad to see fellow detective already at work," Chan noted. "Why, then, call on humble guest?"

Watkins nodded toward the manager.

"Thanks for the vote of confidence, Mr. Chan, but Mr. Krednish and I agreed that with your help there would be no need for the police. And, well, the safe was empty except for—"

"What we need, Mr. Chan," Krednish interjected, "is discretion. I'm sorry to say that the only item missing from the safe is the package entrusted to the hotel by the Winterslip family, and Watkins believes—"

"They were professionals, Mr. Chan," the hotel detective said flatly. "They opened 'er up, took the thing, left a note—" he reached into the safe and extracted a folded slip of paper— "and they want a trade, an exchange."

He handed the note to Chan without hesitation.

"I gave it a quick dusting—no prints."

Chan read the tersely worded demand: *No police. Put $100,000 cash in new valise. Top shelf South Station lost luggage room midnight Friday. Item will be returned.*

Krednish produced a spotless handkerchief and mopped his brow.

"Naturally the hotel wants to avoid a scandal at all costs, and the Winterslip family . . ."

"You think wealthy family would pay large sum to retrieve this object rather than seek guilty party?" Chan said without expression. "What is nature of missing item, and why would pillars of society not desire that justice be done?"

Krednish paused before replying.

"Please understand that Mrs. Winterslip disclosed information to me in the strictest confidence, since secrecy was apparently intended to avoid attracting unwelcome attention from potential thieves . . . I may as well tell you that the item was a valuable tiara, a family heirloom, with several precious gems embedded in it.

"As for your second question, Mr. Chan, in my experience these old Boston families go to great lengths to avoid even a hint of scandal," the manager continued. "It must seem odd to you, a policeman—and one from a vastly different part of the world—"

"Parts of world not so different when wrongdoing is concerned," the detective said pointedly. "People are much the same in that regard."

He looked for a moment at the two men. Krednish was pale—a police matter of this magnitude involving Boston's elite would damage, if not destroy, his professional standing. Watkins lit a White Owl and appeared indifferent—it was still a better beat than any he had walked in former times.

Chan returned his gaze to the penciled note.

"Again, I rudely remind you that I am guest of hotel whose first instinct is that you should consult very fine Boston police department. But since you have decided against that course of action, what is the reason for summoning me here?"

Krednish swallowed before replying.

"I wanted to appeal to you, Mr. Chan, to communicate directly with the Winterslip family . . . to extend the hotel's profound apologies for this outrage, of course, and to determine their wishes. The hotel will act as the family wishes. Of course, if they prefer that we report the theft to the police, we will do so at once."

He hesitated for a moment.

"I can hardly bring myself to mention it, but time is of the essence if the item in question is to be returned in time for the wedding."

"Pardon professional inquisition, but please answer few questions first," Chan returned. "Theft discovered how long ago?"

Krednish glanced at his wrist-watch before replying. "I had just arrived—it was no more than thirty minutes ago—when I opened the office door—"

"Door was locked?"

"Yes, I used my key."

"You saw immediately that safe was empty?"

"Just as I entered the room—I suppose it was on my mind, what with the hotel's preparations for the wedding..."

"Combination to safe known to many of hotel staff?"

"Well—no, I don't believe so."

Krednish paused as though the thought had not occurred to him before.

"The safe predates my time here, and it's impossible to know for certain. But surely you don't think that the staff—"

"You have occasion to open safe from time to time?"

"Rarely. The hotel doesn't keep large sums on hand, so the safe is only used when a guest asks that an item of unusual value be stored securely."

Chan sighed. He had hoped to fulfill his role as father of the bride free from any worrisome complications unrelated to the impending nuptials. But the gods, he realized, must have other ideas.

"I will retain note and make suitable communication to Winterslip family," he agreed. "Beyond that I cannot say what, if anything, this hotel guest will do regarding unusual case of kidnapped jewelry."

CHAPTER VI

A FAMILY DRAMA

Charlie Chan had been looking forward to visiting Boston's Chinatown this day. He was curious to see something of his countrymen's substantial enclave in New England, even though—he had been told—many of them spoke a Chinese dialect mostly unknown to him. Now, he thought regretfully, this personal side trip would have to wait.

Having returned to the family suite from Krednish's office, Chan exited quietly, descending to the hotel restaurant. He broke his fast with tea and toast, then telephoned his son-in-law-to-be to request an audience with Grace Winterslip. It would be best to enlist John Quincy's aid in the matter, he considered.

"Good lord!" John Quincy's reaction to the news moved quickly from surprise to action. "What about it, Charlie—what are we to do?"

"Your mother—she is the owner of this stolen item. The hotel has asked that I communicate with family. If possible, I will come this morning to Winterslip residence," said Chan. "I suggest that you and I discuss this matter in confidence with Mrs. Winterslip. No need to include anyone else, for now."

"Come as soon as you can, and I'll prepare Mother for the—er—unpleasantness of this situation," Winterslip replied. "Thanks, Charlie."

Chan hung up the lobby courtesy telephone and approached the front desk where the manager was registering a newly arrived guest, an elderly woman with a great deal of luggage. Krednish glanced anxiously toward Chan, who waited his turn in silence.

"Mr. Chan—good morning—have you had the opportunity—"

"Good morning, Mr. Krednish, so happy to see you. I am grateful for this opportunity to express satisfaction with hotel accommodations. My entire family are enjoying first stay in ancient city of Boston."

The newly arrived hotel guest smiled at Krednish, collected her luggage and departed, but other comings and goings persisted within earshot. It was not the time for a confidential conversation.

"So pleased to see you here at desk," Chan continued, "so that I can ask you to summon a taxicab, please? I have an appointment to meet my daughter's intended—and his mother. We have much to discuss."

"Oh? Yes—yes, of course, a taxi. Right away, Mr. Chan. I'm delighted to hear that you and your family are pleased with the Statler." He picked up a telephone and dialed. "I hope to speak to you again, soon."

Krednish accompanied "soon" with a meaningful nod. "Yes, further conversation at appropriate time would be welcome," Chan replied blandly. "Will await transportation outside, thank you."

Krednish nodded, and the detective exited the lobby. In a few minutes, a cab pulled up to the curb.

"Louisburg Square, please," Chan told the driver. "Number twelve."

"How nice of you to call, Mr. Chan! I'm so happy to have this extra time with the father of the bride—'to be,' that is."

Grace Winterslip beamed at the detective as though they were old friends. He wondered at this jovial reaction to his visit, since John Quincy had said he would break the news of the theft.

The faithful retainer Greynebin waited on mother, son and detective in the Winterslip parlor, serving coffee and tea before withdrawing.

"I've told Mother about the unfortunate business at the hotel," the younger man began, responding to the detective's puzzled expression. "She's actually taking it quite well."

"Don't talk about it as though I were absent—or senile," Grace Winterslip sniffed. "It's not as if someone has died, and it's hardly a calamity compared to the state of the world today. And as for the wedding plans, well, 'gang aft agley,' you know."

Setting aside Robert Burns, John Quincy forged ahead.

"Now, Mother—anything that you can tell Mr. Chan about the contents of the package would be helpful. There's also the matter of this demand for money, assuming that you want to retrieve this. . . ."

"It's the 'something old' in the wedding planner's guide, you know," she explained to Chan. "The bride should wear, 'something old, something new, something borrowed—' "

"—something blue," the detective finished with a smile.

"This old item, the thief or thieves ask for large sum to return it. Does it have great value?"

"You're very tactful, Mr. Chan—a rare quality in this tactless age. Everyone seems to be so blunt now, extraordinarily so. Hurry, hurry, hurry—"

"Mother—" John Quincy interrupted.

"I know, I know," she snapped. "To business! To put it simply, Mr. Chan, the brides of the Winterslips—sounds like a dreadful cinema presentation, doesn't it?—the bride of each Winterslip has worn this, well, heirloom for several generations at her wedding. After fulfilling this tradition, the 'something old' has been placed in safekeeping until the next generation has need of it."

Chan nodded.

"Many cultures honor traditional customs when two are joined in marriage ceremony. Excuse the vulgar question, but does this item have monetary value in addition to family sentiment?"

The family matriarch seized the opportunity.

"Allow me to answer your question fully by telling you a kind of origin story," she began. "The Winterslip family is among New England's oldest and most prominent—"

John Quincy sighed.

"Did you speak, dear? No? I realize that you've heard much of this before, but Mr. Chan needs the full picture."

Tenting her fingers, Grace Winterslip continued.

"Where was I? Oh, yes! The family—it has a storied history, which I will spare you, except to remark that my late husband's forefathers were ambitious and accumulated significant wealth. Their commercial interests were many—shipping in the colonial days, and a variety of pursuits thereafter.

"Like any old family of means, the Winterslips developed a number of traditions, some of which have come down to the present day. Of these the custom of adorning the family heir's bride, on her wedding day, with a modest symbol of the Winterslip heritage has been observed in an unbroken line stretching back—my goodness, well over one hundred years. That symbol is . . . "

She paused for dramatic effect.

"A tiara."

John Quincy strove to contain his inner plebian, but it was no easy task.

"You mean to tell me that the Winterslips have been crowning their brides for generations with a—a—"

"Tiara, yes," his mother fluted. "A bit ostentatious, as I recall it—almost a circlet, but not quite, of white gold, several good-sized stones—"

"Diamonds?"

"Yes, John Quincy." His mother spoke as one might to a small child. "Diamonds. Crystallized carbon."

"Then the thing must be worth—" John Quincy spluttered. "And that's why there was a police escort—"

Mrs. Winterslip's tone shifted to one of empathy.

"It's no use, son. You've done very well so far, surrendering your common man principles, coming home for this—this wedding—which I'm sure you think of as an unseemly display of wealth. You made your choices in life, San Francisco instead of Boston; more of a worker, a striver, than most in the family. You've been very tolerant of your mother's desire for a grand event."

Her son hastened to shift the conversation from an examination of his views concerning life and society.

"It's quite all right, mother. The more immediate question is: What are we to do about getting it back?"

Charlie Chan had been feeling like an onlooker, observing a family drama that seemed to be about more than jewelry. As for the tiara, he had purposefully refrained from disclosing the limited knowledge that Krednish had shared with him; his intuition told him the matter was better left to the family matriarch to reveal in her own way.

But dealing with thieves—that was something more in his line. It was also, he thought, an opportunity to steer the conversation away from Winterslip filial relations.

"Please pardon this interruption from an outsider," Chan said gently, "but I would suggest that options for retrieval are few. Is head of family prepared to produce the sum demanded . . . and does ransom amount agree with value of the item?"

Grace Winterslip's gaze was aimed at a point over the detective's left shoulder; her thoughts seemed to be elsewhere.

"Retrieval? Getting it back? It's rather difficult to speak of such things—hard to think of something one has only seen once, years ago, as being gone. It's as though it was never really here. As for its worth—that's an interesting question, Mr. Chan."

"No doubt value of family heirloom as such could be considered priceless," the detective replied. "But thieves not so sentimental—so we must consider the matter in more worldly terms. Last valuation of ornament was when, please?"

"That's just it, you see—or more accurately, that's *not* it."

As his mother paused, John Quincy braced himself for a digression, if not a dissertation. His readiness proved justified.

"As you can see, Mr. Chan," she began, gesturing at her own somewhat gaudy jewelry, "I'm no stranger to 'sparklers'—an odious term, I always think—and John Quincy can attest that I've never shied away from wearing them, regardless of their monetary value—really, so common to buy and sell shiny rocks as though they were worth the earth, so to speak—and so, having married into this family, I suppose I can appreciate—"

"I'm sure Mr. Chan would *appreciate*," John Quincy interrupted the soliloquy in an attempt to refocus the conversation. "I'm sure he would be grateful to learn what, if anything, you recall of the actual value. Perhaps the firm that insured the item—you used Benefield, Taylor and Snipes, I assume—they must have had it valued . . ."

John Quincy trailed off, realizing that he was starting to sound a bit like his mother.

"Fine firm, yes; we always use them when necessary," Mrs. Winterslip said brightly. "But not in this case."

"What? Why not?"

As John Quincy girded himself for round two of "Mother vs. Son," Chan interceded.

"Perhaps trusted firm not used because venerable family chose not to insure interesting item," the detective suggested.

"Now, that's remarkable—quite remarkable, Mr. Chan," the old lady beamed. "Your reputation as a detective is certainly deserved. Quite like Sherlock Holmes, or William Gillette, or—"

"No insurance?" John Quincy was puzzled.

"Please pardon intrusive observations," Chan continued. "Family that honors custom once a generation—family represented here by remarkable and unique lady, elsewhere by members who abandon traditions altogether—unlikely to value unseen, unused item highly."

"Quite so, Mr. Chan," Mrs. Winterslip nodded approvingly. "Dear me, are we that obvious? I always fancied myself to be more obscure—or do I mean opaque?"

"Probably both, mother."

Her son smiled and attempted to summarize the main issue's outstanding questions.

"Not to harp on the matter at hand, but where does that

leave us? Are you content to abandon tradition—and the tiara of uncertain value—in defiance of who knows how many generations of Winterslips? Will the guilty go un-punished? Read our next issue for the answers to these and other questions as this exciting tale unfolds!"

"It *is* a bit like a dime novel, isn't it?" Mrs. Winterslip acknowledged. "As for paying the . . . ransom? I know that's the term in the case of a kidnapping, but I assume it ap-plies here as well. Whether or not payment is made—that's really up to you, I suppose.

"Although, as you might suspect, I do have an opinion," she continued. "Legally, however, the tiara has been placed in your keeping—it has come out of the bank, where it was my responsibility, and turned over to you. Thus it became *your* responsibility."

"With all due honor to you—and to all those previous generations of Winterslips—might I inquire, that is to say, what *is* your opinion, Mother?"

"I certainly wouldn't put a large sum of cash toward an uncertainty," Mrs. Winterslip said tartly. "Possibly my ad-vanced age has made me careless of the worldly goods your father bestowed upon me, but I wouldn't give a farthing, tuppence—what's the word I'm thinking of?—a groat, if that's the term. A plugged nickel."

"Lady with extensive monetary vocabulary makes her opinion clear like cloudless sky," Chan put in. "As some would say oppositely, 'money no object.' The same is true in this case. You would prefer that this matter be pursued without regard for return of jeweled item?"

"You put it very well, Mr. Chan. If John Quincy agrees?" The son nodded, and the mother continued. "The family does not regard this as a police matter, and—especially since you are about to become a member of the extended family—it's entirely appropriate that you look into this—these—whoever they are."

Her tone softened a bit.

"Neither my late husband nor I put much stock in the value of 'the trinket'—that's what he sometimes called it—or the idea of the tradition itself," the family matriarch confided. "I suppose we were, in our own way, rebelling against the old ways"—she turned to John Quincy—"perhaps that's where you inherited some of your tendencies, dear boy.

"In any case," Mrs. Winterslip said firmly, "plans for *this* wedding will not in any way be affected by a—a minor incident."

"Not in any way," John Quincy affirmed. "What about the police, Charlie? We don't want to impose on you—our guest, a member of the wedding party—"

"I am happy to be of assistance to family in its time of need," Chan replied. "But report to police warranted whenever serious crime occurs, and value of stolen item points us in that direction."

He paused for a moment; a thought had occurred to the visiting detective.

"Perhaps family of longstanding reputation has one or more police acquaintances who could be consulted?"

Mrs. Winterslip smiled. "How silly of me! I should have thought of this earlier. The commissioner is an old friend. I'm sure I could—"

John Quincy demurred gently.

"Now, mother. No need for that, especially if we would prefer to keep this at least relatively private."

His own memory was jogged by the mention of the highest police authority.

"In fact, I made the acquaintance recently of a police

detective who has already been briefed on this matter—in a manner of speaking.

"I think I will pay him a visit."

"Well, Mr. Winterslip. I didn't expect to see you again. How can I help you?"

Big Mike had steered his visitor into a dingy interview room normally reserved for questioning suspects. Precinct coffee had been offered and declined; John Quincy lit a cigarette.

"It's a bit awkward—thank you for seeing me without an appointment." McCaffrey nodded. "The fact is, we were reluctant to call in the police, so I thought that perhaps I could discuss the matter with you, unofficially . . ."

"We'll see about the unofficial part," Big Mike replied noncommittally. "First of all, who's the 'we' who didn't want to call the cops?"

John Quincy exhaled a cloud of smoke. "Perhaps it's better if I start at the beginning . . ."

The family representative gave an abbreviated history of the missing tiara, including McCaffrey's help in ensuring its safe delivery to the Statler and the subsequent disappearance of the locked box.

" . . . the hotel and the family are interested in avoiding any unnecessary publicity, as I'm sure you understand. The Statler has its reputation to consider, and we—the family—are concerned with the wedding," the Winterslip bridegroom-to-be concluded.

"Big outfit like the Statler—you think they wouldn't worry about a little scandal," Big Mike grumbled. "As for the family—you say your mother don't want to put up the cash?"

"Correct." John Quincy nodded. "We'd prefer that the

matter be handled as quietly as possible, but after talking it over with a friend of the family we, that is, I thought it best to place the matter in your hands."

He smiled inwardly at describing his future father-in-law as a family friend. *No need to bring Charlie into it when he's supposed to be enjoying Boston*, he thought.

McCaffrey considered. Things were quiet at the moment, and since this new wrinkle was tied up to one of the captain's chores, O'Rourke would surely approve of him taking it on.

"So, you've ruled out paying, and you don't want us to go after 'em—at least not officially," the detective summarized. "What you want is for me to poke around, which I can take up with my captain . . . "

McCaffrey snapped his fingers.

"Say! What happens when you don't pay up? Is the family concerned about that? Maybe this—these—whoever they are won't take no for an answer."

"I hadn't considered that possibility," John Quincy admitted. "They seem to be under the impression that the item is so valuable, in more ways than one, and that we can't proceed without it, but that's an error in judgment on their part. The wedding will go on, regardless."

"Well, I guess I have everything I need to look into this a bit," McCaffrey said without enthusiasm. "If you think of anything else that might help, please—give me a call."

John Quincy replied in the affirmative and departed.

Ever since he first walked a beat, McCaffrey had always thought that most of Boston's big bugs were dizzy, and this whole thing seemed to prove it. *Well, it would do no harm to make a few calls, see a few people—and fill in O'Rourke later. It was no big deal.*

He reached for the telephone and dialed.

CHAPTER VII

A NIGHT OF REVELS

Molly Meek had done her best to reassure McGee that all was well, that all would go smoothly, but he was not convinced.

In McGee's view, there was ample cause for concern. The wedding events—plural—were due to begin in a few days: a luncheon, rehearsal, rehearsal dinner, late-night cocktails (for the younger crowd), wedding party breakfast and, finally, the ceremony itself.

McGee's personality included a peculiar blend of . . . Worry? Anxiety? Fear? What she knew of him, Molly considered a bit odd.

"Sometimes," she told friends, "I think the man just ain't right."

At least thirty years old, Aloysius McGee personified timidity. A slight man in frame and stature, he looked every bit the librarian he had once been. His appearance from collarbone to close-cropped hair was positively owl-like, with sharp, beaky features, and large round eyes that observed the world through the round lenses of frameless spectacles.

He still lived with his mother.

Molly didn't understand completely the causes of her fellow clerk's worries but could usually soothe whatever mixture of dread and anticipation of disaster was upper-most in his thoughts at any given moment.

Tonight was different.

From the moment she arrived—unusually early, for once—Molly Meek had responded to her co-worker's real and imagined what-ifs.

"I know what you're thinking," McGee insisted. "I do tend to dwell on what might go wrong, and I'm forev-er concerned about the worst possible thing that could happen. But as my dear old mother says, even a broken clock is right twice a day. Maybe this is one of my times to be right about something."

"Now, then, McGee," Molly reassured him for the tenth time that night. "I'm not saying you're wrong or right. All I want you to do is make the best of things. Whatever hap-pens, no one can fix all the blame on the front desk man."

"It's as though someone or something just isn't quite right here, not as it should be," McGee continued, ignoring the reassurance. "I've been feelin' it for quite some time. I'm sensitive that way, y'know."

"Don't I know it," she grumbled. "I've been hearing all about your sensitivity for as long as we've known each other. I declare, you're a one-man radio receiver, you are."

"Don't kid me, Molly. This is serious. You mark my words, something—Wha-what was that?"

McGee turned his head sharply toward the muffled sound that had intruded on their conversation. Meek glanced in the same direction.

"My word, you're jumpy tonight," she scoffed. "After all this time, you surely know the sounds that fly-by-night elevator makes whenever it feels like it, don't you?"

As if to prove her point, the culprit's doors opened, and Emmet Gilbert emerged.

"Blasted heap of junk," he said with a yawn, seeing an attentive audience of two at the reception desk. "I think it hates me, doing that on purpose after my long day of duty.

"Speaking of which," he continued, "have either of you seen the precious Simon? He's late and I'm tired."

Neither of the clerks had seen the other elevator man and said as much. Gilbert shrugged.

"Then I'm for a nap, right here"—he gestured toward the lobby's inviting furniture—"so that I'll be within call for any guests who need a ride. Let me know when my relief shows up, won't you?" Emmet Gilbert settled himself into a comfortable chair, selecting a copy of the *Evening Transcript* from a side table to cover his face.

McGee prepared to take his leave, cautioning Molly to remain vigilant—for what, exactly, he could not say—and extracting a promise that she would call him if anything out of the ordinary happened.

"Greetings, friends!"

Simon Russum came through the main entranceway just in time to disturb Gilbert's nap and delay McGee's departure.

"How are we all on this pleasant evening?" Russum continued, a trifle louder than necessary given his surroundings. "Ready for a night of revels, filled with—"

"Half-shot and well-oiled," muttered Gilbert from beneath the sports section. "As usual."

Molly Meek sighed. As the clerk on duty, she took charge of the situation.

"Mr. Gilbert—I know it's past your time, but could you please prop him up till I get something brewing?"

The long-suffering Gilbert discarded the *Transcript* and rose. "Sure, sure. But it'll take more than coffee to make this boiled owl fit for duty."

"Say, who you callin' an owl?" demanded Russum, sinking into the chair Gilbert had just vacated. "Did somebody say jamocha? Two lumps of sugar in mine, please—and plenty of cream!"

Molly Meek said something unladylike under her breath and headed for the manager's office to make coffee.

The telephone rang insistently, repeatedly. Reaching out in the dark, Brody Watkins overturned a half-full glass of water, swore, turned on the lamp, and grabbed the still-ringing phone.

"Hello? Yes? Who?"

The voice on the other end spoke rapidly, urgently.

"Slow down—say, what time is it?" Watkins glanced at his wrist-watch. "Ok, ok—just lock the office door, and I'll be right there."

He hung up, rubbed an unshaven chin, and reflected.

Well, there'll be no shortage of those glad to give him a send-off. Molly will be passing a hat for a wreath, and maybe a bottle of Champagne.

These inappropriately callous thoughts intruded on the business at hand—he was the hotel detective, after all, with a job to do. There would be the police to deal with; no doubt they'd already been called. He had best be on his way. Watkins roused himself, wiping up the spilled water with a handkerchief. Dressing hastily, he grabbed hat and trench coat and departed.

CHAPTER VIII

OTHER NOT-SO-ORDINARY THINGS

The front desk and lobby were a sight to behold.

His worst suspicions having come to pass, McGee had remained, all thought of sleep gone from his mind. Gilbert also had stayed, helping administer several cups of black coffee to the suddenly soberer elevator operator.

Simon Russum's jovial mood and tipsy behavior were no match for Molly Meek screaming down the house. He was still a bit groggy, but the discovery of a body, and a hysterical woman, had straightened him up considerably.

Before long, Brody Watkins arrived, and the assembled staff huddled in the lobby at his direction.

"Now, then, who called the police?" Watkins demanded. Blank stares. "Blast it all anyway, none of you thought to call the department?"

Molly raised her head—she had recovered, somewhat—and responded with something more like her customary spirit. "We called *you*, you jughead—ain't you the hotel dee-tec-tive?"

"All you said was, 'lock the door,' so that's what I did," McGee chimed in.

Watkins swore, not for the last time that night.

"Damn your eyes, McGee! Do I have to do your thinkin' for you? Get on the horn to headquarters. Tell them—

you're sure he's dead, Molly?"

"Oh, he's dead alright," she returned grimly. "Nobody with a hole in their head like that is still among the living."

"Ok, then. McGee—Call DEVonshire 1212. Tell the desk sergeant there's been a shooting at the Statler, the manager is dead. That should be enough to get a squad car and a few officers here.

"And while we're waiting," he said, picking up the house phone, "I'm going to ask one of the guests to help out."

Charlie Chan answered the telephone on its first ring. He had not yet accustomed himself to the many time zones of difference between Honolulu and Boston. Although it was quite late, he was deep into a city history, one of the books of local interest supplied to all the guest suites.

Speaking softly to avoid waking family members, he grasped the situation from the house detective's terse description. In a very few minutes he had dressed and joined the gathering in the lobby.

It was a tense group, understandably, and he knew some of them: the front desk clerk, Molly Meek, and one of the uniformed elevator men, Russum. And Watkins, of course.

Chan nodded to those he did not know, looking at all of them for any hint, any expression out of place. This was not his case, but long experience told him there was nothing so valuable early in an investigation as a look at the faces of those on the scene.

The house detective's expression was no mystery; Watkins was eager to consult him.

"Mr. Chan—I'm grateful. I know this is an imposition, I never dreamed when I stopped by to introduce myself that there would be any need—"

"Perhaps there is no need now," Chan replied, bowing slightly. "You mentioned that proper authorities have been notified and are on their way here—what can I do?"

"It's just that I thought I should take stock of the situation, and with someone of your reputation on hand—"

"Please pardon my rude interruption. You wish me to witness your examination of possible crime scene? I am happy to serve as a disinterested observer while you visit the place in question."

"That's fine, then." Watkins was relieved.

Raising his voice, he addressed the staff. "Everyone stay put, the police will be here any minute. They're going to want to talk to all of you."

He pointed behind the reception desk for Chan's benefit and led the way, depositing his trench coat in the lobby cloakroom en route to the office. "It's just down the hall here, around the corner . . . the manager's office. Usually locked when Mr. Krednish isn't at the hotel, but a few of us have keys—"

He stopped at the door, producing a ring of keys from a coat pocket. There were several, and he fumbled for the correct one.

"All these look about the same, the locksmith must've been fond of the manufacturer—" After several tries, the correct choice was inserted in the door and turned with a satisfying click.

"Just a minute, you!"

Behind Watkins and Chan, a small police parade had rounded the turn in the corridor; two uniformed officers and a rather large plainclothes detective approached.

"I'm McCaffrey, from headquarters," the police detective said. "You're Brody Watkins, right? I remember hearing about you."

"That's right, I'm house detective here," the little man offered. "This is Inspector Chan of the Honolulu police. He's a guest at the hotel. We were just about to take a look—"

"Sure, sure." McCaffrey said noncommittally. "You two," he said to the two uniformed officers, "back to the lobby and keep those people there—and don't let anyone wander down this hallway. And another thing," he called to their retreating backs. "Keep an eye out for the medical examiner, and send him along when he shows up.

"I'll trouble you for that key, Watkins, and just step aside for a moment if you would," McCaffrey continued.

The house detective complied, pulling the door open and moving two steps back to make way for official authority.

"It'll be better if I have the first look at things," McCaffrey said, stepping into the doorway, "and I can see there's not much room for a whole committee."

As the police detective had observed when he first visited Krednish's office, the windowless room was barely more than a converted closet. On that occasion, he had merely delivered a package; this time, he took a greater interest in the office and its trappings.

There was space enough for a small desk and chair, which faced the doorway, a few shelves containing books and office bric-a-brac, and a tiny side table with hotplate and coffeepot. The wall behind the desk was cheaply paneled, with a rectangular mirror hanging at eye level.

The unfortunate occupant was seated behind the desk, slumped forward onto its top. Ledgers and papers lay across the desktop, as though the manager had been hard at work when death interrupted.

The police detective drew a deep breath and let it out.

"Mr. Chan, I've read something of your work over the years. If you wouldn't mind taking a look with me—?"

Nodding, Chan entered the office close behind McCaffrey. Watkins peered through the doorway.

"You can identify this man?" McCaffrey turned to the house detective.

"Yeah—that's Krednish, alright. He's—he *was*—the manager, and this is his office. No question."

McCaffrey reached into the dead man's inside jacket pocket and withdrew a wallet.

"I.D. card says Braxton Krednish, et cetera," he informed the others. "Not much else—a few dollars. No driver's license?" He turned a questioning look toward the house detective.

"I don't think he had an automobile," Watkins said helpfully from the doorway. "Lived somewhere close by and walked to work. Say! Look there on the floor." He gestured toward McCaffrey's scuffed shoes. The police detective stooped with some effort and picked up a pawn ticket that lay where it had apparently fallen.

Charlie Chan was examining the top of the cluttered desk. Ledgers and bulky files rested under the dead man's hands and head; white papers shone spotless from the light of a banker's lamp; two telephones occupied the desk's right side. A small 12-month desk calendar, a full ashtray, and a black metal deed box competed for the remaining space.

Watkins pointed out the box, which was open.

"Better check that black box—that's where he kept petty cash, and any other money on hand," the house detective put in.

McCaffrey was examining the body; his unofficial observer delved into the metal container.

"Box now like winter bird's nest," Chan pronounced.

"Empty."

"Maybe this was a robbery gone wrong," Watkins said. "I told him not to keep a lot of cash on hand, but he would do it."

McCaffrey had taken only a cursory look at the body.

"Looks like a single gunshot to the top of the head, high on the forehead. Can't tell for sure without moving the body, but I don't see any signs of an exit wound, and I don't see a gun here."

He stood up and scratched his head.

"We'll need a formal ruling from the coroner's office, but to me it sure looks like homicide. Medical examiner can tell us about the cause of death for sure."

Watkins was quick to chime in; after all, this was his hotel.

"I'd say it looks like someone came in and caught him at work. He must've been looking down at—" the hotel detective gestured at the items under the dead man's hands—"all of that when somebody came to the door, quiet-like, and squeezed off just the one shot. Easy enough to do, the office is so small that you could do it from the doorway—right about where I'm standing."

"One moment, please." Chan interjected. "Guilty visitor arrives quietly and shoots man without first asking for money? And why kill if robbery was only motive?"

"Maybe somebody wanted Krednish out of the way," McCaffrey offered, "and the cash—assuming there was a lot of dough in the box—was just—"

"Happy accident for person who shoots? Possibility cannot be dismissed," Chan replied. "This manager—who would have benefitted from his removal, who were his enemies? These are questions for you, Detective McCaffrey. Murder without motive is like mouse that makes friends with cat. Possible, but unlikely."

McCaffrey shrugged. "We'll know more after we talk to some of the staff." He gestured toward the body, desk and office. "Do I read this setup right, Mr. Chan?"

"Early indications agree with your assessment," Chan replied. "Your medical examiner can confirm cause of death, extract bullet from body."

He paused.

"Dead man's professional surroundings may tell stories, too."

"Anything stand out?" McCaffrey's tone was hopeful.

"Contents of office present many possibilities for your investigation," Chan began. "My opinions at present useless, like chimney until fire is lit."

"Yeah, well—about that—" McCaffrey glanced at Watkins. "Brody, would you mind? Give us just a minute."

"Sure, sure," the house detective closed the door, leaving McCaffrey and Chan alone in the cramped office.

Big Mike McCaffrey cleared his throat.

"Mr. Chan, I don't mind telling you that I'm new to this business. Been pounding a beat till just last year. And, well—"

He paused to collect his thoughts. Chan waited.

"Truth is, I just barely made detective. Two months ago. Been cooling my heels ever since, just doing little jobs for the captain, 'chores' he calls them. It's like he's expecting me to be a washout before I can show the department what I can do. And now this—it could be a chance for me to . . ."

It was an awkward moment. Charlie Chan waited, but it was clear that Big Mike could not bring himself to simply ask for help.

"This death, so unfortunate for victim and hotel, presents professional opportunity for you," Chan began.

"I am here in this city with family, to serve as father of the bride in wedding—in just a few days. I have no authority, no official standing.

"But," he continued quietly, "many years ago I was as you are now—seeking same professional opportunity, a chance to prove capabilities. And I was aided by senior officer.

"Perhaps I could help—unofficially—as you pursue solution to this case. You are in charge, success when it comes will bring you credit. I remain in background, thinking intently and taking separate path to truth. We divide this investigation, like cutting apple in half to see where is the worm inside."

Big Mike looked relieved.

"I was hoping you'd agree to something like that, Mr. Chan. It's not that I want you to do my job—I just want to learn from you, and maybe get a leg up in the department. These days, it can be hard for a guy like me to get ahead. I get the feeling the captain thinks I'm all heart and no brains."

"Captain maybe has too many who would learn and not enough time to teach." Chan remarked. "Learning is like river—begins with small streams that eventually join their waters. We pursue different avenues of inquiry, compare notes, combine results. I am helpful hotel guest, and at all times you are in charge."

"Thanks—thanks very much." The big detective reddened slightly; he was not used to unburdening himself, especially to a stranger—and a famous stranger at that. "Enough about me and my problems. I'm going to go talk to some of those people in the lobby."

"Will join you shortly," Chan said. "One suggestion—make sure office is locked. Need to keep unauthorized persons, curious people, from disturbing scene of wrong-doing."

Big Mike opened the door; Watkins, leaning against the wall, hastily put out a stubby cigar. "Mr. Watkins, here's your key —Inspector Chan is going to take a few minutes inside, and you need to lock up when he's done."

"Sure thing," cried the hotel detective. "Mr. Chan, I am at your service."

With Watkins in tow, Chan turned his attention to the office and desk.

Having noted the desktop clutter earlier, he looked more closely at the ashtray's contents. Beside a few cigarette stubs, a long, thick cylinder of ash reposed in the round, black receptacle.

Nearby, a small upright desktop calendar was out of date in two ways, he noted, picking it up for a closer look. All twelve monthly pages were intact; neither January nor any of the subsequent months had been torn off and discarded.

"He wasn't the most organized guy I've ever come across," Watkins noted. "Not to speak ill of the dead and all that, but how could you keep track of what's going on in the hotel with this mess of a desk?"

"Also hard to 'keep track' of hotel without accurate record of time—in days, months, even years," he observed.

"What do you mean?"

As the two men stood behind the desk Chan pointed to the calendar, which he grasped gingerly by the edges to avoid disturbing possible fingerprints.

"Days pass one after the other, yet calendar does not keep up. Observe." He indicated the topmost month. "Not only is January now long gone, but so too has 1930 faded into history. Very curious, someone has altered correct year."

Watkins peered at the annual record and saw on January's page that the year at the top was indeed "1930" due to an inked-in zero.

"You got me, Mr. Chan. What's the point?"

"Small things sometimes tell big story," Chan replied. "For now, this one only worth noting—along with any other not-so-ordinary things."

"Such as?"

"Several call attention to themselves, I think." Chan grinned. "No doubt fellow detective has already noticed them, so I will not point to them now. Also, disorganized items on desktop may yield clues on closer examination."

Watkins rubbed his unshaven chin with a forefinger, a habitual gesture. As Chan scanned the desktop, the house detective leaned over the body and looked down.

"Say, look there—some of those papers on the floor next to his feet—"

Chan knelt and reached carefully over the dead man's legs to retrieve several documents. But another object caught his attention. Without comment, he wrapped it in a pocket handkerchief and slowly got to his feet.

"Something in those papers, Mr. Chan?"

Chan gingerly pulled aside the handkerchief to reveal a revolver, holding the end of the barrel up to his nose briefly. "Weapon fired recently, it appears."

Watkins whistled. "He kept that gun around in case of trouble, he always said. Maybe we were wrong about this, Charlie—can I call you Charlie?—the whole set-up looked for sure like somebody took care of Krednish and then scooped the cash, but his own gun, maybe he—"

Charlie Chan rewrapped the gun and deposited it in a side pocket, silently absorbing the growing array of indications—too soon to call them "clues," he knew from experience—seemingly pointing in differing directions.

Murder planned by someone who desired money? Unplanned murder and coincidental theft of cash in plain sight? Suicide by unfortunate manager for reason to be determined—followed by theft? *Or*, Chan thought ruefully, *perhaps empty cash box was already in such a state before this Krednish met his end.*

"Mr. Chan—er—Charlie?" Watkins broke into Chan's seeming daydream respectfully. "What do you think it means?"

Chan set aside his thoughts for the moment.

"Like bites of food for the famished, each discovery increases our appetite for more facts."

"I get it—always more to find out in a situation like this. I remember a case when I was with the department, we thought for sure it was murder at first, and it turned out we was wrong, because—"

"Excuse this interruption, please." Chan interjected politely. "Before more time passes, I suggest that we join official police to hear their questioning of hotel workers."

The two men exited the office, and Watkins locked the door.

CHAPTER IX

"AN INTUITION ABOUT TROUBLE"

"Don't you open your big trap about things that are none of your business!"

Simon Russum was mostly sober now, and the elevator operator resented any hint that his work was not what it should be. His ire was directed at Molly Meek, who had referred in passing to the unsteady nature of the hotel elevator—comparing it to the equally uncertain demeanor of its operator. McCaffrey's lack of experience was showing; he was trying to gauge the attitude of several staff members by questioning them en masse.

"Pipe down, rummy." This from McGee to Russum, who responded by aiming an unsteady punch at the desk clerk's head. McGee ducked with little effort, and Big Mike stepped between the two.

"Enough of that, now, or I'll knock some heads together," he snapped. "Everybody just settle down till I have a chance to talk to each of you."

Complaints and some swearing arose from all sides. The hour was late, and it was clear that fatigue and hunger were uppermost in the minds of those assembled.

"Detective McCaffrey, one moment please," Charlie Chan, with the house detective in his wake, had arrived at an opportune time. Standing behind the reception desk, he leaned toward Big Mike and spoke in an undertone.

"Perhaps better if we adjourn this group to hotel dining room. Hunger and cooperation are strangers to each other. Even at this time of night, surely food and drink can be provided—and we can question all those present, in calmer mood."

He pulled the wrapped gun from his pocket.

"Here, for police to examine, is recently fired weapon retrieved from floor near dead man."

McCaffrey took charge of the gun, and Watkins—who had been listening at Chan's elbow—stepped forward to address his fellow hotel employees.

"Folks, I know some of us have been here past our time, and we're all a little on edge now. Mr. McCaffrey is just doing his job, and I'm sure we all want to help him get to the bottom of this. How about we head to the restaurant for some grub—and some coffee?"

This suggestion met with general approval. The grumbling subsided, for the most part, and the weary group headed down the hall to the restaurant where the Chan family had dined more than once.

Charlie Chan took McCaffrey aside, "Permit me to remark that gun at feet of dead man betrays odor indicating it has been fired recently, and your ballistic experts may find comparison with fatal bullet instructive. Also," he went on, "in questioning these persons we should 'play dumb,' as son Henry would say, and ask about recent mood of this manager, and whether he kept any weapon in office."

"Good idea," McCaffrey nodded. "None of these people have seen the body, so let's not show our hand—let's see what they say." He smiled broadly. "Anyway, I'm real good at playin' dumb."

"Also, I have simple suggestion to shorten long night

for all," Chan said quietly. "Let us do as ancient generals advised, divide and conquer these persons. Then we can share their words—this little talk is only a beginning, of course. The single step that begins a long journey."

"That's fine, Mr. Chan," the detective replied as Chan ordered two of the hotel workers to a table on one side of the room and the other two a table on the opposite side.

"I'll take this side of the room," McCaffrey pointed toward Emmet Gilbert and Simon Russum, "and leave the other two to you."

Chan nodded. He joined the cafeteria line and obtained a cup of tea before approaching the clerks.

"You permit that I join you for conversation concerning the night's events?"

McGee shrugged. "Don't see that we have much choice," he whined.

"McGee! Where are your manners?" Molly Meek scolded her co-worker, who shrugged it off. He was used to it. "Please have a seat, Mr. Chan, and tell us how we can help," she said. "What would you like to know?"

"Thank you so much." Chan settled what he sometimes referred to as his "avoirdupois" into a dining chair designed for lesser mortals.

"I regret the need to subject you both to questions about the unfortunate event." He paused to take a sip of tea. "To begin, please, recount evening's happenings from the moment you arrived at hotel."

He nodded at Molly.

"Lady first, if you would be so kind."

Molly Meek sighed.

"I tell you, these nights all run together after a while. Let me see . . . tonight, I mean last night, I got to the hotel a little late—McGee here, he wasn't any too happy with me," she said ruefully.

McGee confirmed his displeasure with a grunt. The woman resumed her story.

"It was busy late into the evening, several folks checked in. McGee stayed on to help out for a bit, then he went to the office to talk to Mr. Krednish about something."

"What time, please?"

"Oh, I suppose it was before midnight, but I didn't pay much attention." She smiled. "McGee usually skips out without saying goodbye—well, you do, don't you?"

McGee started to speak, but Charlie Chan interrupted.

"Please—you will have opportunity to describe events when lady is finished." He turned back to her. "Manager Krednish often kept late hours?"

"Sometimes—he was more likely to be there at night than first thing in the morning, but he worked long hours— you never knew when he was going to show up."

"When he appeared at work in recent days, did he seem as usual?" Chan's pocket notebook came out, and he jotted down a few particulars.

"I suppose so." She paused. "He always seemed to have something on his mind, and there was always a problem or a situation that he had to deal with."

"Many in hotel work keep some weapon nearby to guard against robbery. Manager here, did he do so?"

"Not that I know of, but he could've done. I never saw such a thing in the office anyway."

"Who else did you see last evening, please—people that you know and work with?"

"Well, in between guests comin' and goin' and asking questions, I wasn't keepin' close track of everybody in the evening. Later on, you understand, things quieted down."

"Any persons you can recall, and maybe approximate

time they were present, early or late—those recollections would be most helpful," Chan suggested.

"Well, I mentioned McGee, I saw him; and Mr. Krednish. Mr. Watkins, he was making his rounds like he always does, and he stopped by to chat."

She frowned for a moment, but a sudden recollection brightened her expression.

"And—oh, yes! I remember now. That was the night when Emmet Gilbert—he's the elevator operator most days—when he had words with Mr. Krednish. I could hear them both all the way out at the desk.

"Then the door slammed, out comes Mr. Gilbert, and right after that—Mr. Watkins, he was passing by—he went back to the office, and I could hear him talking to Mr. Krednish—and Krednish, he was still talkin' loud. I heard him say, 'That Gilbert,' just after Mr. Watkins went back there."

She paused, glancing across the room at Emmet Gilbert.

"Then there was another fella—I don't know if he was staying at the hotel or not—but he came up to the desk. Said he wanted to talk to Mr. Krednish real bad. So I told him to wait till Watkins was done, but he couldn't wait. Took himself off before Mr. Watkins come out."

"Did this man leave his name?"

"No—he was upset and in a big hurry."

Chan nodded. "You said Emmet Gilbert and manager have noisy conversation. Same true for talk with hotel detective?"

"Oh, no. Mr. Krednish, he was swearing about 'that Gilbert' at first, but then I heard him speak to Mr. Watkins polite-like. About that time, I remember the elevator went thump, and then I saw Emmet take some guests up."

She cleared her throat and paused for a sip of coffee.

"Anyway, Mr. Krednish and Brody—Mr. Watkins—

they talked a while, and Mr. Watkins wished him a good night when he left, so that was all right."

"Mr. Watkins left for other duties, or did he depart hotel?"

The woman's brow furrowed.

"Seems like it was getting pretty late when all that happened. I believe he went out the main doors, he may have said, 'Goodnight, all,' but I was talking to a man who was checkin' in about that time. It's hard to remember exactly what happened when."

"Understandable," Chan replied. "Events of evening crowd together like waves of ocean—hard to tell where one ends and another begins."

Charlie Chan offered the clerk a nearly identical menu of questions, but McGee yielded little additional information. He confirmed Molly Meek's impression of the manager as a perpetually stressed man dealing with the hotel's constant problems and situations.

No, he had not noticed anything unusual in the dead man's demeanor; he had not seen, nor was he aware of, a weapon—a gun, a knife—in the office. The most dangerous thing he had seen in Krednish's possession was a wicked-looking paper-knife that the manager sometimes used to open the mail.

"I must tell you," the clerk offered, "that I have felt for quite some time that something was going to happen, that something was out of sorts—"

"Here you go again—always frettin' and never satisfied till somethin' bad happens!"

Molly emitted a gruff snort of contempt.

"Don't you listen to him, Mr. Chan. He's always sayin' that trouble's on the way, and then when it comes, it's, 'I knew it all along—I told you something bad was coming.' " The woman's mimicry of McGee's fretful style was near perfect.

McGee flushed angrily. "Sure, sure—have your fun. I tell you I have an intuition about trouble, and sometimes I just know when it's on its way. I may not always be right, but this time, I was."

The friction between the two clerks was evident. Chan wondered: good-natured banter inflamed by the situation, or some deeper conflict? This relationship, he thought, deserved further consideration—but not now.

"Frequent listener can hear sour notes in familiar song even during skilled performance," the detective observed. "Thank you both for answering questions about unhappy event. One last question—was any unusual noise noticeable, perhaps gunshot, during the hours in question?"

Both clerks shook their heads. "Gunshot?" Molly exclaimed. "The elevator makes a big noise every so often, usually when Gilbert's on duty, but that happens so much I don't pay much attention."

"Elevator announce its presence in that manner last night?"

"To tell the truth, I don't know one way or the other," she replied. "Between the elevator thumpin' and the office door slammin'—I can't say which noise was what."

"Are we free to go?" McGee demanded. "I need some shut-eye before Molly's shift is over."

Across the room, Detective McCaffrey had just received a note from a uniformed officer.

"We're all through here—for now," Big Mike told the four hotel workers. "But let's not have any of you leaving town, for business or pleasure," he warned. "We'll be in touch."

Emmet Gilbert, Aloyisius McGee, Molly Meek and

Simon Russum departed, and McCaffrey joined Chan to swap stories.

"Nobody saw anything, and nobody heard anything," the police detective summed up sarcastically. "Everybody was so busy minding their own business—how could they hear a gun go off?"

"Witnesses often behave like children confronted with empty cookie jar," Chan noted. "The crime is indisputable, but no one knows anything."

Big Mike laughed.

"Ain't it the truth? I guess that's one of the things that makes this line of work . . . interesting."

Chan smiled.

"One small correction, please—not everyone knows nothing. From those questioned, I learned of angry words between victim and elevator operator Emmet Gilbert. Strong words between Gilbert and victim indicate ill will— worthy of further exploration. Detective Watkins, perhaps, overheard end of this argument and may be able to shed additional light on nature of dispute."

McCaffrey rubbed his chin. "Not everybody loved Krednish, that's for sure. I'd love to talk to this Gilbert more, one on one. And maybe some of the others can shed a little light on the bad blood between the two of 'em. And speaking of Watkins, where did that bird get to?"

"Hotel detective absented himself from our interview session," Chan replied. "Perhaps to attend to nightly duties.

"For now," he continued, "I suggest that more talk with suspects—and others who are not suspects—will reveal more than they wish to share," Chan agreed. "We have several possible roads to take, like travelers at start of journey."

"Well, the first trip I want to take is back to that office for a closer look—care to join me?"

The two rose, and Chan looked at his wrist-watch. "Poets say night is long, but this one grows short," he observed. "Nonetheless, I am happy to join you."

CHAPTER X

"ON THE SUBJECT OF TOBACCO"

Apart from the body's absence—the note Big Mike received confirmed the medical examiner's crew had removed it—the office appeared unchanged. For the two detectives, the chief feature of interest remained the cluttered desktop's assorted work materials, full ashtray, telephone, monthly calendar and the open (and empty) cash box.

"The boys dusted the room—found prints from the victim, the reception-desk clerks, but nothing else," Big Mike said. "Nobody in the hotel we talked to seems to know the combination of the safe—or so they said, anyway."

"Possibly manager Krednish committed that information to memory alone, but he may have left a reminder in case of failure to recollect necessary numbers," Chan said thoughtfully. "Even though earlier theft means safe is likely empty now, it would be useful to discover if some hidden guide to opening it was discoverable by others."

"No arguments from me, but how's a fellow to find the right numbers?"

McCaffrey flipped open a bulky ledger by way of demonstration.

"There's nothin' *but* numbers everywhere you look," the police detective asserted. "He might've put the combination on one of these bookkeeping pages so he could find it sure and simple—but to anyone else, it would look like just another row of figures."

"I am thinking of simpler method, one that hides in plain sight." Chan picked up the little one-month-per-page calendar he had puzzled over previously. "Possibly these strange markings on guide to current year, page after page. Suggest you open mirrored door and we try experiment with hidden safe."

McCaffrey complied.

Standing close by, Chan pointed to the "1930" with an inked-in zero covering the correct digit. "Many safe combinations start at zero. Rotate knob three turns clockwise—and then begin at that most valueless number."

Mystified, Big Mike twirled the knob as directed, coming to rest on zero.

"Now what?"

Grasping the little calendar with one hand, Chan began to turn the pages so that McCaffrey could follow along.

"After starting at zero, we turn pages to look for more curious markings. January, nothing. February—observe, please—the 'r' in February is circled in same color ink as the zero in 1930, and so is the eleventh day of this winter month. From zero, turn dial right to eleven."

Big Mike complied. Light was beginning to break.

Chan had been flipping through the rest of the year's pages; the remaining numbers of the combination were revealed, and McCaffrey followed instructions until a satisfying "click" indicated that the safe was unlocked. Big Mike swung open the door.

Empty.

Chan returned the calendar to the desktop while the police detective looked closely at the vacant space.

"Well, I guess I'm not surprised, Mr. Chan, but I had

hoped that something in that safe might give us a clue. Say—it was smart work, figuring out that combination! My hat's off to you."

Chan grinned. "Detecting sometimes like dog digging up ancient bone—what one man hides, another man may discover."

"That's for sure." McCaffrey laughed. "Sometimes I wish there were a few more bones to find—is that what you're looking for now, another one?"

Chan was going through the desk as though searching for something. "One item of possible evidence to collect," he replied, extracting two slim glassine envelopes from a drawer.

Using one of the manager's calling cards as a makeshift shovel, he carefully transferred the contents of the ashtray into the two envelopes, carefully separating cigarette ends from what he could collect of a long finger of dark-gray ash that lay apart from the lesser stubs and their powdery remains. He deposited the envelopes in an inner coat pocket.

A knock at the door announced the house detective's return.

"I figured you two would be here," Watkins said. "Find anything else?"

"Unlike in popular fiction, dead man did not leave solution in sealed envelope," Chan replied. "As real-world police often say, 'We pursue multiple leads and look forward to solving case soon.'"

He turned to McCaffrey. "That is the usual statement, yes?"

McCaffrey nodded. "It sure applies to the current situation, Mr. Chan."

Brody Watkins grinned. "Sounds good to me. Say, before I forget—I wanted to pass along some dope I picked up from Gilbert, Emmet Gilbert—the daytime elevator operator. I know you just talked to him, but did he mention his beef with Krednish?"

McCaffrey shook his head, but Chan nodded affirmatively.

"Same was communicated to me by Molly Meek," he told Big Mike, "and I apologize for failure to mention argument when we compared notes."

"That's ok, Charlie," McCaffrey said. "What interests me is that Gilbert conveniently forgot to tell me about it."

Watkins seemed to savor the moment: He had discovered even more information and was contributing to the investigation.

"Well! Let me fill you in," the little man said importantly. "Seems these two had a history. I won't bore you with the details, but as best I can gather from what the staff have been saying, Gilbert had it in for Krednish—hated him like poison. Played little tricks on him from time to time, banged the elevator into the lobby, things like that. Talked about him to the other staff, how Krednish was goin' to get his—that kind of thing."

"Talkative staff indicate reason for contempt?" Chan queried.

"No, not exactly, but Krednish, Gilbert and Russum worked at the old Parker House hotel. That is, they worked there—until they didn't. One of 'em had a little trouble with upper management. It seems Krednish was assistant manager there, Gilbert and Russum were elevator operators. Anyway, so the story goes, the three of 'em left about the same time. Krednish bounced around for a bit till he landed here, right away he hired Russum, who was lookin' high and low for a job. Not long after that, Gilbert ended up here, too."

Watkins tugged at an earlobe. "What I can't figure is why."

"Why what?" Big Mike was puzzled. "Why all the bad blood with those three?"

"That too," Watkins replied. "One of 'em got the other fired, that's what I figure. No, the 'why' I can't understand is why both those elevator operators ended up here. Krednish didn't have to take either one of 'em on. Then, Gilbert, the ungrateful so-and-so acts—well, ungrateful! Why knock a man who's keeping you outta the poor house?"

"Perhaps conversation with ungrateful elevator operator will shed light on feud of many years," Chan put in. "First, I have errand to perform. Sorry to say that I did not bring quantity of tobacco to city—assuming I could purchase same here. Hotel, perhaps, has tobacco shop?"

"A little one, just off the main lobby," Watkins replied. "But most of the guests go down the street—it's just a couple of blocks—to a shop called Crestwark's. I've been there a time or two, the man there stocks all kinds of smokables."

Big Mike McCaffrey entered the tobacco shop with Chan following. The opening door nudged a bell that announced their arrival, and the proprietor sprang up from his seat behind the counter like a five-foot jack-in-the-box. He and the shop suited each other somehow; dressed in a fashion twenty years behind the times, the little man maintained a certain elegance: from his patent-leather shoes with spats to a shiny bald pate. In between, a gold watch-chain peeped from a dark vested suit. A discreetly patterned tie was restrained by a celluloid collar.

He had seen fifty some years go by with the aid of the gold-rimmed pince-nez through which he now gazed at these two potential customers.

One who indulges in the noble weed, one who does not, professional intuition told him. *Policemen or attorneys no doubt.*

The shop's worn and comfortable atmosphere consisted mostly of shelf-lined walls brimming with tobacco-filled jars. Blends from many countries, though separated by their clear glass enclosures, collectively presented visitors with an aromatic League of Nations. Its members included Virginia tobacco and pleasantly pungent representatives from India, Turkey, China, Brazil and elsewhere.

"Good day, gentlemen," the tobacconist piped. "How may I serve you?"

Big Mike produced his shield. "I'm McCaffrey from the department, and this is Mr. Chan, who's working with me. We're investigating a certain matter and would like to ask you a few questions about cigars."

"Pleased to make your acquaintance." The proprietor blinked rapidly, and the corners of his mouth turned up slightly.

"My name is Crestwark, and this is my shop. I have come to know a few things about cigars over the years," he said modestly. "I have a variety in stock—my humidor's substantial capacity, you understand . . . What questions may I attempt to answer?"

McCaffrey nodded to his unofficial consultant. "All yours, Charlie."

Chan produced the glassine envelope, holding it gingerly between thumb and forefinger.

"In this container we have collected remains of certain cigar, one consumed completely as it reclined, unattended, in ashtray. I do not indulge, but have noted how those who prefer cigars to cigarettes often must apply flame repeatedly."

He handed the translucent envelope to the tobacconist.

"Two questions, if you would be so kind. Unattended cigar that burns completely, leaving only column of ash—would such be of an unusual type? Second question: Can you determine, like so many detectives of fiction, type of tobacco from sample of its ash?"

The little tobacconist received the glassine container with all due reverence. Opening it carefully, he examined the contents—without removing them—with a large magnifying lens, humming a tuneless string of notes to himself. It was a kind of anti-melody of his own devising that indicated a professional challenge had caught his fancy.

"Interesting—very interesting." He looked up quickly. "May I remove a sample?"

"Please," Chan replied. "We would be greatly interested in expert opinion."

Humming all the while, the tobacconist extracted three samples with a small spoon-like instrument, depositing them separately on a metal tray that he had pulled from beneath the counter. Removing the pince-nez, he looked closely at the little heaps of ash; first with the handheld lens, then with a jeweler's loupe that materialized with the speed of a conjurer's trick.

McCaffrey had not read Conan Doyle in his youth, and this interest in tobacco ash was a bit too esoteric for him. Spying an ashtray at the end of the counter, he lit a cigarette and glanced at his wrist-watch. It would be lunchtime soon, and that place on the corner near the station house had a special he had been meaning to try—

"Hah!"

The detective's brief bout of woolgathering was interrupted by the tobacconist's exclamation.

Chan had been watching the proceedings with great

interest; scientific methods were a passion of his. "You have observed something of particular interest?"

The tuneless tune had resumed as the tobacconist returned to his close examination. It took him a moment to recall the presence of his customers.

"Something of…? Yes, indeed, Mr. Chan." The little man smiled broadly, revealing not one, but two gold-capped teeth. "Quite so. Remarkable, even.

"What we have here is, I would say, ash from an expensive, and probably quite old, Honduran cigar—definitely not Cuban; no, indeed. You see"—his gaze shifted from the ash to Chan, one eye enlarged mightily by the loupe—"most people think of Cuba as the world's most venerable cigar producer, but that's a bit of an exaggeration."

He removed the loupe, gesturing with it.

"All across that region, of course, the cultivation of tobacco is quite old, but there are certainly, hmm, local differences. Yes, indeed. Variations in climate and soil, first—then, cultural traditions that have affected, shall we say, the quality of the finished product. In Honduras, the tradition of cigar-making is many, many hundreds of years old—more than a thousand years old, in fact … "

There was a great deal more in this vein, but eventually the tobacconist drew closer to the matter at hand.

". . . as for the provenance of this particular sample of ash, gentlemen . . ."

The two detectives leaned forward expectantly.

". . . it's difficult to say."

McCaffrey swore, inwardly. Unperturbed as always, Chan persevered.

"Would such a cigar that produces this ash be sold here—or elsewhere in this city?"

"I'm embarrassed to say that my humble shop does so

little trade in such—such rarities as this, by which I mean; well, my customers have fine tastes, and I have an extensive selection, but—"

"Cost of items such as this lie beyond their means," Chan supplied. "Especially during this time of difficulty for so many."

"You put it very well, Mr. Chan," the little man said promptly. "I would go even further, beyond speaking for my loyal and occasional customers, and tell you that none of my fellow tobacconists in the city regularly supply cigars likely to produce this ash."

His tone and expression as he uttered the words "fellow tobacconists" reminded McCaffrey of a man he had seen the other day scraping something foul from the sole of his shoe.

"As to your first question—I haven't forgotten it, you see!—the common, inexpensive cigar often does require repeated lightings. You described a cigar, apparently lit once and left in a horizontal position, in an ashtray, resulting in a single column of ash."

He paused and replaced the pince-nez, the better to focus his gaze on his small but attentive audience.

"I have known of Honduran and Cuban cigar-makers whose creations would behave in such a manner—without becoming too technical, it has to do with the blend of tobaccos used in the wrapper, binder and filler. The Corojo, developed recently in Cuba—"

"Thanks for not being too technical," McCaffrey broke in, trying unsuccessfully not to sound sarcastic, "but I gather that our sample came from an expensive cigar—one you probably can't get in Boston for love nor money. Does that just about cover it?"

"Yes, indeed," the tobacconist replied, oblivious to

McCaffrey's impatience and deaf to his sarcasm. "Assuming that your sample of ash was collected locally, I'm sure that the cigar in question was brought here by a well-to-do gentleman, someone of refined tastes, perhaps a traveler visiting the city."

"Expert knowledge welcome, like spring rain on parched earth," Chan told the little man. "We must not take up any more of your valuable time, but is there any other item of information—no matter how small—that you would share with us?"

"Oh, my—on the subject of tobacco, even on cigars alone, I could write a book. In fact, I plan to do so," Crestwark replied enthusiastically. "In my idle hours, I have begun to set down the beginnings of what will surely be the most significant work on the subject since—since . . ."

Swept away momentarily by a rosy vision of authorial fame, the little man suddenly realized that he had lost his audience.

"I beg your pardon," he muttered, coloring slightly. "Got carried away. You gentlemen— you're more interested in this ash sample than my literary aspirations, of course.

"I would add one final thought, somewhat speculative on my part," he continued. "It concerns the portion of the sample here"—he pointed toward it with a nicotine-stained forefinger—"where you can see, if you look closely, a discoloration at variance with the rest of the ash."

"So?" McCaffrey had learned enough about tobacco for one day, perhaps for a lifetime.

"I know it doesn't seem like much," the tobacconist said apologetically, "but, you see, it's a different color because it's not tobacco."

"What was it, then?" Big Mike's curiosity was stimulated.

"The maker's label, the cigar band," the little man announced triumphantly.

McCaffrey was mystified. "I don't follow you. So what if the label burned up—I mean, you can't tell anything about the manufacturer from that, can you?"

"No, no—indeed, no." Off came the pince-nez, and the tobacconist produced a handkerchief from a hip pocket. Cleaning the lenses, he continued.

"Cigar-smokers come from all walks of life. The common man enjoys a good smoke just as much as a captain of industry. But"—he wagged the glasses toward his audience, then put them onto the bridge of his nose—"a man who seeks out and purchases cigars of a certain quality, like the one that produced this ash—that man would *not* leave the band in place as he smoked it. For a fine cigar such as this, it's customary to light up and, after a few minutes, remove the band.

"Of course I may be imprudent in drawing any conclusion, but it seems to me very likely that the person who lit that cigar was either exceedingly careless or simply ignorant. Perhaps a person who had come into money recently and was unused to the finer things. In short, a man whose previous taste in cigars was more . . . pedestrian."

The detectives thanked Crestwark and exited the shop. McCaffrey lit a cigarette; he sometimes smoked cigars but somehow had lost any appetite for them just now.

"Little man combines eye for detail with enthusiasm of an expert for his chosen subject," Chan remarked. "You found his conversation enlightening?"

Big Mike believed in reducing complicated matters to the essential.

"I'd say we're looking for a man, probably from out of town, who's come into a packet recently. He can afford to buy an expensive cigar—and he didn't buy it in Boston, according to our friend, so he made his money somewhere else, bought a fancy cigar, and probably some new clothes and so on, and came to town. He's either staying with friends, or—since he's livin' the high life with his new dough—he may be lodging at one of the higher-class hotels."

"Like the Statler, perhaps?" Chan suggested. "Maybe he stays there, in luxury suite, and calls on the unfortunate manager to renew old friendship, or to conduct business."

"Possibly, possibly," McCaffrey admitted. "Or he might've lived in Boston his whole life and just took a trip somewhere—and that's where the cigar came from."

"Many possibilities worthy of exploration," Chan replied. "I have great interest in brief exploration of documents at city's hall of records, then, perhaps, a talk with certain hotel staff—perhaps you could examine hotel registry? Suggest you look for names of men traveling alone, especially any man from large city.

"Maybe visiting stranger arrive in hotel with both expensive cigar—and keen desire to meet man who now lies dead."

CHAPTER XI

BREAKFAST AT CALLAHAN'S

"Next!"

The clerk at the counter—a Miss Letitia Wagenstern—never speculated about the peculiar and diverse reasons that drove people to delve into events long past. For her, it was enough that each request was fulfilled, each person in the line met with and dispatched quickly, with minimal fuss.

Charlie Chan approached the counter, removing his hat and bowing slightly. Even in the most mundane circumstances, whatever the setting, he always observed the courtesies due to others.

"Good morning. Would like to see, please, vital records for this city from nineteenth century," he requested.

Miss Wagenstern suppressed a sigh. "Could you be more specific? Our records are organized in the usual categories—marriages, births, deaths, real estate transactions, wills . . . and each of those occurs in bound or filed collections of documents—and each category according to years, decades—"

"Only marriages and births, please—for period from 1870 to 1920," Chan specified.

"Are you interested in any particular family name or, shall we say, letters of the alphabet?"

"Experienced keeper of records is most astute," Chan smiled. "Those records for persons whose last names begin with the letter 'W,' please."

"Between our cross-referenced system and each volume's indexing, you should be able to find what you're looking for quite easily. One moment."

The clerk vanished into a library-like office interior only partly visible to those waiting in line and returned in a few minutes with four large volumes on a cart. She slid the big books, one at a time, over the counter to the waiting detective. "Please take these to one of the tables and return them to the refiling cart when you've finished with them."

Chan transferred his weighty research materials to an empty table and was soon immersed in Winterslip pairings and blessed events from the Victorian era to the dawn of the Jazz Age. Ignoring the temptation to explore each and every branch of the family, he speedily identified events of potential interest: the marriage of John Quincy's grandparents, the birth of their first child, Grace's husband; the year of Miss Minerva's arrival (later than Chan had assumed); and the younger sister Rose had told him about—who it was said had left home and died young.

Two items of possible interest were worthy of noting in Chan's ever-present notebook. The birth of a male infant Winterslip, no first name recorded, caught his eye. Also, the ill-fated Cora had, it appeared, married quite young—an aspect of her story of which he was unaware.

"Playing a hunch," as cousin Willy Chan was fond of saying, he perused the marriage records further, in search of . . . he knew not what.

It was shortly after midday when Chan returned to the family suite, finding only a hotel housekeeper making beds and tidying up.

"Please pardon this interruption of your duties—it is hard work to restore order to many untidy rooms," the detective said, noting the rounded shoulders and careworn face of the middle-aged maid. "Every night I see fruits of your labor and have marveled at efficiency of those who perform this service."

"That's very kind of you, sir, and we do take pride in a job well done," the woman replied. "It's not just me, o' course, there are four young girls—young in my eyes, anyway—but they all do well, and I try to keep all of us organized."

"You are, then, the head housekeeper—Mrs.—?"

"Brennan. That's right, sir." Her speech featured traces of a County Mayo origin. "Glad to have worked my way to such a position after many a year spent scrubbing floors and I don't know what-all."

Chan nodded sympathetically.

"Noblest works are often humblest tasks," he said kindly. "In position of responsibility you have no doubt already heard unfortunate news of manager's death?"

The woman nodded.

"Perhaps hotel news travels so quickly that you also know I am assisting police—helping to investigate?"

"Sure, and the whole staff knows you're a detective from foreign parts," Mrs. Brennan replied. "That is, from the islands with the strange name—beggin' your pardon—and the girls have informed me that the—the—those islands aren't foreign at all, so. . ."

Interrupting this summary of territorial nomen-clature and political status, Chan pointed to the suite's ashtray, in which more than one of son Henry's cigarette butts reposed.

"Question, please, related to investigation. Many guests practice tobacco ritual?"

"Smoke? I should say they do," Mrs. Brennan exclaimed. "A filthy habit, I always say—hopin' that you yourself—"

Chan assured her that smoking was not among his faults and continued.

"All kinds of tobacco consumed on premises by guests and staff? Cigarettes, pipes—cigars?"

"Cigarettes, by far," the head of housekeeping replied. "Even some of the women, and it's shocking to see. Of all that worked here, only poor Mr. Krednish—God rest his troubled soul—smoked a pipe.

"Cigars," she continued slowly, taking mental inventory. "Mayhap a handful of guests the last few days, and none of the staff, as best I can recall."

"Hotel has room for smoking? Perhaps free smoking materials are provided for guests there?" While not a smoker, Chan had stayed at hotels where such was the case.

"There's the men's lounge, but why it's called *that* these days is a fair puzzlement to me," Mrs. Brennan exclaimed. "Men *and* women smoke in there, more often in the evening than at other times of the day. And the hotel matches—the little books with the name on the cover— that's all that's given away. Them that's needin' somethin' to smoke must go to the hotel shop or down the street to the tobacconist."

"Have just returned from visit to Mr. Crestwark's interesting establishment," Chan replied. "I am grateful for your patience with my many questions. Answers will be helpful in pursuit of truth."

"Very glad that I could be of help," the woman replied. "If there's nothing else, I'll be taking my leave—yours was just the first room on my rounds this afternoon, so—"

"Would like to make strange request, if you would be so kind," Chan interrupted. "Is it possible that you could collect cigar stubs from ashtrays of rooms you visit—making note of each room and name of cigar-smoking guest?"

"Garnies!" Mrs. Brennan was taken aback, but recovered quickly. "It's a bit of a tall order, to be sure—"

She was interrupted by the insistent ringing of the room telephone. Chan crossed the room quickly to answer the call.

"Mr. Chan? This is McCaffrey. I'm down at the station and just turned up a bit of news about one of our friends at the hotel. Do you know what time that elevator man—the other operator, Russum—d'you know when he comes on duty?"

"Not for several hours, I am thinking," Chan replied. "Is he someone of interest in death of manager?"

"Maybe." Big Mike's voice boomed through the earpiece. "But what the records have turned up is more about that other matter—look, since he's not due there for some time yet, let's go see if he's at home to visitors, for a friendly chat. I can fill you in then."

McCaffrey supplied the elevator operator's address; Chan jotted it down in his notebook.

"I will join you there shortly," he said, and hung up.

"Excuse untimely interruption of our conversation," Chan said to the cleaning woman who was putting the room to rights. "Possible for you to collect items mentioned earlier?"

"Well, sir, as I was sayin'—I don't know that it will be an easy thing to do, but I'll speak to the girls and we'll get what we can. Shall I leave it all with the desk clerk?"

"Thank you so much for taking on important task. I ask that you return materials to this room, please, so as not to disturb work of busy person at reception desk."

Opening the room door to depart, the detective turned and grinned.

"I may be pursuing untamed waterfowl, but he who hunts unlikely bird sometimes catch same."

Big Mike McCaffrey was waiting at the curb as Chan exited a taxi at the elevator operator's rooming house address. The neighborhood was not one of Boston's finest, but the row houses were mostly respectable in their outward appearance, and the location was fairly close to the hotel.

"It seems this Russum has had some experience in the jewelry trade," Big Mike informed Chan as they mounted the front steps. "Enough so that he would have the knowledge, maybe, to be very much interested in what was in the hotel safe. Connections, too," he continued, ringing the doorbell, "of a kind that would be helpful in turning stones into cash."

The door opened abruptly, revealing an unkempt woman of uncertain age who cast an unwelcoming eye on the two detectives.

"Well? What is it now? Whatever you're selling, I have no need for it—and no time to waste—"

McCaffrey's badge stemmed the tide of objection long enough for him to get a word in.

"Good day to you—my name's McCaffrey, this is Inspector Chan. We're looking for one of your boarders, Simon Russum. Is he at home?"

"Oh, that one," the woman scoffed, brushing back a graying strand of hair. "You'll not find him here at this time of day. He's 'breaking his fast,' as he calls it. Although his idea of breakfast usually comes in a glass."

She pointed down the street.

"Try Callahan's place—it's on the corner, you can't miss it."

As the two men turned to look toward the direction indicated, the door slammed shut. The interview, evidently, was over.

Callahan's public house was nearly deserted at this hour, and the detectives found their quarry seated in a booth, doing justice to a plate of ham and eggs—washed down by a glass of rock and rye.

"Gentlemen, gentlemen," Simon Russum greeted them with an airy gesture. "Won't you join me? I can recommend a breakfast cocktail—juice of the orange, fruit of the . . . grain, as you might say. Sweet and satisfying, and the eggs aren't half bad."

McCaffrey and Chan seated themselves opposite the hotel worker. A waiter brought coffee for Big Mike; Chan declined food and drink.

"So, now," Russum pushed aside his empty plate, re-lighting a half-consumed cigar. "How can I help you gentlemen this fine day?"

Both detectives glanced first at the cigar, then at each other.

"That's, uh, quite a cigar," McCaffrey remarked, wrinkling his nose at the stogie's malodorous bouquet. "Where do you get them?"

Russum stared at the police detective. "What th'—you tracked me down to ask me about cigars?" He blew a small cloud of pungent smoke out of one corner of his mouth. "I get my tobacco here and there—there's a shop on this block, and the place near the Statler."

"Any particular—brand? Cuban? Honduran?"

Mystified, the hotel worker shook his head. "I like variety. And I don't go in for the fancier ones. I ain't exactly John D. Rockefeller—a good five-cent cigar is good enough for me." Russum discarded a gray heap of ash on the floor; McCaffrey pushed the ashtray toward him.

"Perhaps others in hotel prefer finer tobacco products?" Chan suggested.

"Say, this has something to do with the goings-on at work, don't it?" The elevator operator was not yet fully awake; he had consumed two rock and ryes; and, as even his closest companions admitted, he was not possessed of a great intellect. "But-but the manager smoked a pipe, and—"

"Speaking of the goings-on at the hotel," McCaffrey seized the opening, "tell us about your professional life before you began taking people up and down at the Statler."

"Nothing much to tell," Russum shrugged. "This and that. Why do you ask?"

"Maybe you had some experience in the jewelry business?" McCaffrey asked, ignoring the question about the question. "At Stowell's, on Winter Street, f'rinstance? And one or two other places, after things didn't go so well there?"

"Now, hold on—j-j-just a minute," the jeweler-turned-elevator-operator stammered. "Sure, I worked there, and I left there, and a few other places, too. So what?"

"So maybe you stayed in touch with some of your pals, and maybe you learned about a certain item at the hotel, an item that was in the keeping of the manager—"

Russum swore. "You can't pin that robbery on me. I didn't do it, and I wasn't there when it was done."

"Not where when deed occurred?" Chan said sharply. "How do you know with certainty when event occurred— if you were not there?"

Crushing the cigar end in the ashtray, Russum flushed. "I'm just sayin'—I didn't do anything, and I wasn't in the vicinity whenever somebody did what they did." His tone was increasingly heated and emphatic. "I didn't hear anything, and I didn't see anything."

McCaffrey remained stone-faced, but Chan grinned. "Like the three wise monkeys that imitator Japanese borrowed in ancient times from Confucius—you see and hear nothing evil. But what about third monkey, the one who speaks no evil?"

"I got nothin' bad to say about anybody, if that's what you mean," Russum returned. "In fact, it's time I was on my way to work, so if you gentlemen will excuse me—"

Flinging a few dollars on the table, he donned a faded cap and marched out of the establishment. Chan's grin faded. "Like stone statue, blind, deaf-and-dumb man sometimes see and hear more than he speaks."

"He sure seems a likely one, to my way of thinkin'," the police detective remarked. "Motive—he seems like a fellow who's always on the lookout for the main chance, somebody who hopes to make a big score. And with that shady history in the jewelry trade, you can bet he'd know how to turn that tiara into dollars and cents."

Chan nodded. "Also true that man who comes and goes from hotel at all hours, one who also travels up and down in elevator, had plenty opportunities to participate in unfortunate events—at the very least, to see or hear something of importance."

"But like most of the citizenry—leastways the ones of his kind—talkin' to the police is the last thing they want to do," McCaffrey said. "I'm for lookin' at the hotel records to see who's checked in these last few days, so you're welcome to join me. But where does our talk with this Russum character leave us?"

"Same place as always," Chan smiled encouragingly. "When obstacle presents itself, we seek alternate path. The road is not always easy, but the destination may not be far off."

"A damned sight too far for my liking," Big Mike grumbled. "I just hope we get there before somethin' else happens."

"Well, hello, little lady! Do your folks know where you are?"

Brody Watkins was used to encountering all manner of stray and wandering hotel guests and visitors in the wee hours—drunk and dazed, lost and confused—but children on the loose in the middle of the day, or at any hour, were a rarity.

Evelyn Chan had returned to the end of the corridor where a few nights ago she had seen—so she said, anyway—"the lady." The girl's exploration was just getting underway when the hotel detective appeared from around a corner.

"Who are you, a policeman?" The girl stared at Watkins cautiously, but unblinkingly.

"Say—you're one of Mr. and Mrs. Chan's daughters I'll be bound," Watkins exclaimed. "Now, then, missy. What's a little lady like you doing, gadding about by herself?"

The girl considered the house detective's line of inquiry; she was used to adults treating her like a child as she looked younger than her teen years. She decided that posing a question of her own was the best policy.

"I remember now—you're the hotel detective who came to see my father," she began. "Have you seen an old lady in the hall on this floor?"

"An old—" Watkins scratched his head. "Lots of 'em. Old men, too. Coming and going all the time. I guess they all look old to you, the grown-up people, that is."

"Not regular people staying at the hotel," the girl scoffed. "The lady I saw was—different, somehow. Like she didn't belong."

"Everybody belongs somewhere, as I'm sure your folks have told you. Now, you run along—scoot back to your room, or wherever you're supposed to be."

Watkins went on his way, and Evelyn Chan returned to the family's suite in search of her father. Unfortunately for Evelyn, he was not in evidence, and she was just in time to join—unwillingly—a family outing organized by her older siblings.

"It's time we all saw something of the city—besides this old hotel," Henry, the oldest, had declared. His mother had agreed, and the older children helped take charge of the younger. Only the bride-to-be and her father were missing; each of them had other matters to attend to.

Over Evelyn's objections, the majority of the family departed for a walking tour of nearby historic sites.

Charlie Chan had no time for a family outing. Having returned to the family suite in time to wish the walkers well, he descended to the lobby in search of McCaffrey, who had accompanied him as far as the lobby.

On his way down, Chan was one of several hotel guests on the elevator—and Emmet Gilbert did the honors. The detective was reminded that a talk with this second elevator man was in order—perhaps during or after his shift.

Exiting the elevator without incident—strange how the machinery behaved itself in varied ways, Chan thought—he presented himself at the front desk, where Aloysius

McGee was on duty.

"Good day, Mr. Chan. How can I help you?" McGee appeared more alert and erect than he had previously presented himself to the detective. Chan wondered at the seeming change.

"I am deeply interested in hotel register—perhaps Detective McCaffrey also has made a request for same?"

"Yes, that's correct," McGee replied. "You'll find him in the office. I'm sure you know the way."

Chan found the detective seated at the late manager's desk, scanning recent guest entries and jotting names and room numbers in his notebook.

"You have found items of interest, perhaps?" Chan inquired. Looking up from his task, the police detective nodded.

"Of the guests who arrived in the twenty-four hours leading up to the murder, I think these three would be a good place to start," McCaffrey said.

He closed the registry and rose from behind the desk.

"Let's go pay them a call."

CHAPTER XII

UNINVITED MIDDAY VISITORS

"Beg pardon, Mr. Winterslip." Greynebin extended an envelope on a silver salver. "Telegram for you, sir."

"For me—here?" John Quincy tore open the envelope, and a smile replaced his puzzled expression. While his mother was elsewhere with Rose, discussing one of the seemingly (to him, anyway) countless details, John Quincy was taking tea with his aunt.

"A congratulatory message for the bridegroom from one of his youthful cronies?" Miss Minerva twinkled.

"You're partially right—but this is good news in an even more interesting way, possibly." John Quincy's cryptic reply hung in the air for a moment.

"Any reply, sir? The Western Union man asked that I inquire." Greynebin waited impassively.

"Yes, by gad!" The younger man scribbled a few lines and handed them to the butler. "Perhaps the Bard was right—maybe journeys do 'end in lovers' meeting.'"

"What on earth are you talking about? If you're going to spout Shakespeare at this hour, shouldn't it be a bit more appropriate?" His aunt raised an eyebrow in mock dismay. "Perhaps something from *Romeo and Juliet*."

"Hardly! The bodies pile up at the end of that one, and what's in my mind is far more cheerful."

Miss Minerva toyed with a small figurine on the mantel, eyeing John Quincy. He seemed in high spirits today—pre-wedding giddiness?

"A young man—that is, a man on the cusp of middle age—but one still capable of giddy behavior," she mused. "Could it be that you have some schoolboy prank in mind, a gentle poke in the eye for your stodgy old family, something planned for your wedding day?"

"Not exactly," John Quincy replied with a mysterious air. "Let's just say that a Winterslip family surprise is in the offing."

"When we encounter each of these three, please question closely about business in this city, sights and sounds observed in hotel, especially around time of recent events—and observe whether he smokes—cigarette, cigar, pipe," Charlie Chan said quietly as he and McCaffrey made their way down the second-floor hallway. "I will look innocently around the room while you talk to each. Have already enlisted housekeeping staff to collect samples from as many rooms as possible."

"Samples? Of tobacco? Seems like a long shot, Mr. Chan—I mean, well, lots of people smoke," McCaffrey shrugged.

"Not only tobacco products, but ashes from same," Chan replied. "Freely admit slim chance of success, but sometimes long shot can be short cut to solution."

"Here we are—room 264." Big Mike knocked on the door, firmly, three times.

"Yes?"

The word and the opening of the door happened simultaneously. A well-built man of at least forty stood in the doorway, his right hand rubbing his cheek. Six feet tall and fair-haired, he appeared to be dressing to go out; he had clearly interrupted the knotting of a striped necktie to open the door.

"Mr. Willis Anderson?" McCaffrey read from his list and produced his badge.

"Police? Yes, I'm Willis Anderson. What can I do for you"—he glanced at Chan—"gentlemen?"

"Perhaps brief conversation better suited to hotel room than public hallway," Chan suggested.

"Sure, sure—c'mon in." Anderson opened the door wide, straightening his necktie as the two detectives entered. His face broke into a wide grin. "Am I a suspect in 'The Case of the Missing Towels and Ashtrays'?"

McCaffrey acknowledged the jest with a faint smile. "No, nothing like that, Mr. Anderson. My name's McCaffrey, and this is Inspector Chan."

"Pleased to meet you both." The big Midwesterner shook hands vigorously with both men. "Sorry I can't offer you much hospitality, but I'm on my way to a meeting—"

"We won't take up much of your time," Big Mike interrupted. "Just a few questions, if you don't mind." He flipped open his notebook.

"Sure, sure—always glad to help the police in their work. It's my first time here, in Boston—first time traveling this far east, in fact."

McCaffrey peppered his subject with questions while Chan stole glances around the room.

"You're from Kansas City—here on business?"

"That's right."

"What kind of business?"

"I'm a glorified version of what they used to call out west a 'whisky drummer,'" the big man grinned. "Wholesaler of liquor and other products."

"Other products?"

"Tobacco, mostly—cigarettes, cigars, chewing tobacco, pipe tobacco, pipes, spittoons in brass—"

"You travel with samples?"

"Wel-l-l . . . not so much this trip." He turned to an over-sized leather valise on the floor next to the bed; Chan had noted it earlier. Anderson flipped the latches and opened the lid.

"I hope you're not thirsty—all I have with me are smok-ables." He gestured toward the contents of the sample case: it was packed full of dozens of cigars, packs of cigarettes—even a few cans of Prince Albert—that filled the room with the sweet, earthy scent of a humidor—or an entire cigar shop.

"Say, that's real handy for you," McCaffrey remarked. "Anytime you need a smoke, you can just reach right in, and—"

"Oh, no—not me," Anderson broke in. "I'm the rare bird that doesn't drink, doesn't smoke. Well, hardly ever." He smiled broadly. "I do swear from time to time."

"Must be hard to convince people that you've got the best quality goods when you don't even take so much as a pinch of snuff."

"It can be a challenge," the big man admitted. "What I do, see, is just quote the experts. 'Finest quality plug tobac-co—best cigars from the Caribbean and South America—most popular cigarette brands on the market today—'"

"You get a lotta call for fancy cigars these days?" McCaffrey's tone was casual, but Charlie Chan looked on intently from across the room.

Anderson shook his head, slowly. "Sadly, no. Oh, peo-ple *say* they prefer a fine cigar—they just don't want to pay for it. That's what the retailers tell me. I do carry a few of the pricier types with me"—he reached into the packed case, gently lifting and rearranging items.

"Well, shucks. Thought I had two or three of the top-notch ones handy, but I can't seem to lay my hands on them at the moment. You gents prefer cigars or cigarettes?"

McCaffrey accepted a slim sample pack of domestic cigarettes; Chan declined. "Thank you for kind offer, but I do not indulge."

"You and me both," Anderson replied. "Well, now, if there are no more questions—"

"Just one or two more," McCaffrey promised. "You checked in the night before last, right?"

"That's right. About seven-thirty or quarter till eight, I think."

"We're talking to guests of the hotel who arrived around that time to see if they noticed anything that seemed— unusual."

"Unusual?" The big man wore a puzzled expression. "Like what? I mean to say, I've never been in a big city this far east before, so I don't suppose I know what would be usual—and what would be out of the ordinary."

Big Mike turned a beseeching eye toward Charlie Chan, who took the hint.

"Cast thoughts back to that evening. You arrived at front entrance; then what?"

The Kansas City man frowned briefly, concentrating.

"Well, now. I took a taxi from the train station—that driver, he made the trip in record time; nice fella, he even carried my bags into the lobby. I checked in at the desk, talked to the man there—"

"What man, please?"

"I think he was the manager—he mentioned that the clerk had stepped away for a moment, and I believe he said that he was just filling in. Real nice fella, asked me about Kansas City, real friendly."

"You observed or encountered other hotel workers, arriving guests, perhaps?"

"Not really. For a big-city hotel, things were pretty quiet, and I was just beat from the long trip—couldn't wait to get to my room. Other than the fella at the desk and the elevator man, I don't remember seeing anybody at all."

His flatlander accent compressed the two words into something like "uhTALL," an expression Chan had not heard before. He was still working to interpret the Boston patois, and now he was experiencing the moderate twang of the Midwest. Punchbowl Hill was far off, indeed.

McCaffrey was satisfied. "Well, thanks for the time. We'll be running along." He turned to Charlie. "Anything else, Mr. Chan?"

"Glad to have made acquaintance of traveler from middle of vast country," Chan bowed slightly. "Most interesting profession—in your travels do you distribute samples freely, cigars perhaps, to those you meet—in this hotel, for example?"

"Good gracious me—not on your life!" Anderson replied. "If I did that on a long trip like this I'd be totin' an empty case long before I met up with the folks I hope to do business with." He winked. "I make an exception for the police—always happy to hand out a few cigarettes—maybe even a cigar— to support law and order."

McCaffrey took note of Chan's satisfied expression, and the two detectives took their leave of the man from Kansas City.

"On to our next customer, 'Cleveland Armitage.' He's just two floors up—shall we take the stairs?"

Chan nodded, reluctantly, and they headed down the

hall to the stairs.

"I guess Mr. Willis Anderson is on the up and up," McCaffrey remarked. "Kansas City is a long way from Beacon Hill, and he doesn't seem like he would have anything to do with this whole business. Unless you saw something in the room—or made more of his answers than I did?"

Big Mike's voice echoed in the stairwell as Chan hastened to catch up—he was a few steps below the younger man.

"Unused hotel ashtrays in room indicate tobacco salesman told truth when he said he does not consume his own wares," Chan puffed, stopping on the landing to catch his breath. "Lack of telltale odor in room confirms that he does not smoke—at least not within that confined space."

McCaffrey had resumed his ascent, taking the last flight of stairs two at a time. Chan followed more slowly.

Cleveland Armitage didn't respond to the first series of knocks, or the second. McCaffrey glanced at the third name on the list.

"Sanchez is just a few doors down this hallway. Maybe we try him and come back to Mr. Armitage—"

As though taking a cue from the sound of his name, Cleveland Armitage opened the door.

"Well?"

The single word conveyed a world of meaning. The smartly dressed youngish man—thirty, perhaps, McCaffrey thought—was going places, had no time for trivialities such as uninvited midday visitors, and was going to be less cooperative than the gregarious Midwesterner they had just encountered.

"I'm Detective McCaffrey, this is Inspector Chan—we'd like to ask a few questions—"

"Ah, the police! Well, well, well—please, come in."

Armitage's brusque demeanor in the doorway failed to improve at the sight of McCaffrey's badge as he ushered the detectives into a replica of the hotel room they had just left. "What can I do for you two . . . officers? Detectives? Always happy to be on the right side of the law."

Cleveland Armitage—"Cleve" to his business acquaintances—had the dark, chiseled features of a matinee idol, and the thin strip of a mustache sported by many an actor of the silver screen. Completing the portrait of a cinematic leading man, his immaculate attire consisted of a two-piece suit of the latest fashion and all the appropriate accoutrement, down to matching tie, pocket square and carnation, signet ring and expensive watch.

"This won't take long," Big Mike assured him as Chan began a surreptitious examination of the room and its visible contents. "We're just talking to some of the guests who arrived in the last few days—trying to get a handle on an unfortunate incident—"

"What a polite way to refer to a murder," Armitage interrupted. "Yes, Detective—McCaffrey, was it?—bad news travels fast in a place like this. The room service boy, the maid, the elevator operator—they've all had something to say about it.

"I assure you," he continued with a smile, "that I am not in the habit of doing away with people—God knows I've had to deal with a few hotel employees—not here, you understand!—that deserved an early departure from this life, but I resisted the temptation."

McCaffrey was annoyed. "Mr. Armitage, this is a serious matter—a man is dead, and we need to get some answers."

"Of course, of course," the oily dandy assured him. "Only too happy to cooperate. How can I help?"

"You're here from New York, I believe." Out came McCaffrey's notebook. "Business or pleasure?"

"Both, always—I try not to separate them completely. To do so would be dull in the extreme."

"But this trip to Boston—is it more one than the other? What's your line of work?"

Armitage cast a sidelong glance at Charlie Chan, whose bland expression concealed his mental stock-taking of the room's contents.

"I have many interests—the theater, for one. You could say I'm a patron of the arts, a collector, an investor—so many things. I often come to Boston, and on this particular occasion there are one or two shows I've come to see—for professional reasons—at the Colonial and the Shubert, and perhaps a few other venues."

His attempted smile was more like a leer; Big Mike suppressed a growing urge to punch him.

"You arrived night before last—about what time?"

"I don't recall the exact time, perhaps before ten o'clock. The front desk clerks—one was, I think, arriving, and the other was leaving work as I was checking in. There was a good deal of chaff back and forth between them."

"Pardon this rude interruption, please." Chan had apparently finished sizing up the room and its occupant's belongings. "Would you happen to have cigarette or cigar—and the means of lighting same? I left mine in hotel room."

Armitage smiled politely, and drew a single cigar from an inside breast pocket. "I'm afraid this is all I have—I don't indulge, normally, but occasionally a business associate will press a cigar on me as a kind of goodwill gesture, and I can't refuse."

Chan held up his hand, politely. "Very kind—but I

would not deprive you of gifted item."

"Are you quite sure? Well, it's just as well," Armitage held the cigar under his nose and inhaled. "I'll give it to some eager hotel employee when an opportunity presents itself."

The man with many interests returned the cigar to his pocket, and McCaffrey resumed the line of questioning—with little result. Nothing out of the ordinary had been seen, heard or sensed at the time of arrival. Encounters with other hotel guests and employees, Armitage told them, were few—and ordinary.

Big Mike may not have been impressed by his interviewee's appearance and manner, but he had no concrete reason to doubt his veracity. The two detectives concluded their questioning and moved on.

Guillermo Sanchez was tired; it had already been a full day, and his evening engagement was likely to be a long and challenging one. The knock at the door was unexpected—and unwelcome.

"Yes? Who is it?" His hand went swiftly, reflexively to a hidden shoulder holster.

"Police. We just want a few minutes of your time."

"One moment." Sanchez relaxed his grip and quickly scanned the room. All was in order. He glanced in the mirror and saw a handsome man, not yet fifty—graying at the temples—clad in the uniform of a professional, gray suit and conservative necktie. *An innocent and hardworking man of business, one who welcomes a visit from the authorities*, he thought, grasping the doorknob and opening the door in a single movement.

"Yes?"

"McCaffrey from headquarters, this is Inspector Chan. You're Guillermo Sanchez, correct?"

"That's right. Please, come in." He closed the door behind them. "Won't you sit down? I would offer you refreshment, but—"

"Thanks, but we won't take up much of your time," McCaffrey broke in. "We're just talking to a few guests as part of an investigation into a few incidents at the hotel."

"Incidents?" Sanchez offered a suitably worried expression. "Nothing serious, I hope?"

"Serious enough. A man is dead and a valuable item has gone missing."

"Dear me—how extraordinary! One reads of such things happening, of course, but—"

McCaffrey plowed on. "As I was saying, this will just take a few minutes."

As the police detective queried Sanchez, Chan looked on—and around the room, as he had previously. All was in order, but something seemed out of place.

"Chinese are psychic people," Chan had often said, or perhaps it was simply a "hunch," as his cousin Willy Chan would put it. Whatever it was called, the sense of . . . evasion, even deception, was present.

Sanchez told Big Mike that he had noticed nothing untoward upon arrival, that he was in Boston "for a few days" to visit friends and see something of the city—it was his first visit.

"You wrote in the hotel registry," McCaffrey said, consulting his notes, "that you are a resident of Washington, D.C., *and*"—glancing at Chan—"Havana. So . . . which is it?"

"It is, as I wrote in the book, both. You see," Sanchez said airily, "I am attached, as it were, to the Cuban embassy. Depending on my duties, and as events dictate, I divide my time. Of course," he said with a smile, "I prefer to be in

Havana during your winter months. Washington weather can be most inclement."

"Pardon this interruption, please," Chan put in. "As one who has wrestled with mighty English language, I congratulate you on skillful use of same. Could it be that you have spent much time in this country?"

"You're very perceptive—Mr. Chan, is it? I had an unusual youth by American standards. My mother was Cuban, my father was an American importer. In Miami, in their house, my mother spoke only Spanish to the children, and from our father we heard only English.

"But this family history is not helpful to you gentlemen! Tell me, what other questions do you have for me?"

Chan played his hunch.

"Most interesting to hear of remarkable parentage. Your father—his business brought goods from other countries to this one—what kind of products?"

Sanchez raised an eyebrow. "Many things, over time, but chiefly tobacco leaf and tobacco products—especially cigars, which I'm sure you know are much sought-after in this country and elsewhere."

"You inherited, perhaps, a fondness for the famous product of your father's homeland?"

"Indeed, yes. I enjoy a good cigar now and then," came the puzzled reply. "But surely you did not come here to inquire into my personal habits?"

"Please forgive my curiosity—no disrespect was intended."

Chan turned to McCaffrey, who resumed the usual line of questioning, eliciting a series of negative, and mildly impatient, responses.

"I don't want to cut short our most interesting conversation, gentlemen," Sanchez remarked, "but I do have an engagement—"

"Not at all, not at all," McCaffrey reassured him. "Thank you for your cooperation—Inspector Chan?"

The two detectives made their exit, and McCaffrey exhaled noisily in impatience.

"What did we get from all of that? I'm all for shoe-leather detective work, but . . ."

Charlie Chan was deep in thought. Big Mike had noticed that the older man sometimes fell into a reverie, a silent interior discussion with himself. Yet Chan remained aware of all that passed in his presence during these ruminations.

Unaware that he was under Big Mike's observation, Chan offered a cryptic reply.

"Maybe one link, maybe two—those we may have collected from visits to visiting travelers."

"Links? Come again?"

Chan grinned. "Assembling clues to arrive at solution slow process—like blacksmith makes many rings of iron before forging chain.

"Soon, we will connect links to construct shackles for guilty."

CHAPTER XIII

RESIGNED TO THE SITUATION

Miss Minerva Winterslip's flinty demeanor, worthy of her Puritan ancestry, had served her well. She had weathered many storms and steered clear of youthful entanglements, content—or so she thought—in her chosen roles, those of Boston doyenne and family matriarch. True, the latter role was one she shared with her sister-in-law, but Miss Minerva took a secret pride in the fact that she—she alone—was truly a Winterslip. The blood of the old sea captains ran through her veins.

Beneath the gruff exterior, memories of romantic youth surfaced from time to time—and this was one of those occasions. Preparations for Rose and John Quincy's wedding, and all the attendant "happily ever after" sentiment, she told herself—that's what was causing these—these unprofitable thoughts!

Her mind wandered from the old century's final decades, when she had first encountered a handsome young officer, to more recent times, when their acquaintance had been renewed. He had made it known that it was not too late, despite the passing of many years, but she had hesitated—and the moment had passed.

She sighed and steeled herself for this last day of preparation; tonight, the inevitable rehearsal—thankfully, she had no role in that, other than that of onlooker—dinner with the wedding party. Tomorrow, the big day; then, life would return to normal.

Nothing can prevent those who plan a wedding from seeing it through—not even a mysterious death. Rose Chan and John Quincy Winterslip, especially Rose, were naturally focused on the impending event to an extent that sheltered them from the worries of those investigating a mere murder. Others were less fortunate.

McCaffrey was increasingly determined to bring matters to a head, but the number of suspects and their possible motives was bewildering. Interviews with hotel staff and guests—he saw possibilities here and there, but nothing concrete—nothing he could get hold of, like when he'd collared many a guilty mug on his old beat.

By their mutual agreement, Charlie Chan had kept his own counsel, but perhaps, Big Mike thought, too much reliance on Chan had been a mistake. In darker moments, the detective doubted his own abilities—this was his first significant case, and it could very well determine his reputation and his future in the department.

From the ground floor's front desk to the top floor's hospital suite, Statler employees were keenly aware that a killer had moved among them. Even though no one had been arrested, and some refused to believe anyone they knew and worked with was capable of such an act, most proceeded nervously about their duties the afternoon before the ceremony. Rightly or wrongly, many assumed that the guilty party was someone they knew—someone whose professional demeanor and personal behavior masked the willingness to kill.

Someone, they thought, who might kill again.

* * *

The happy couple and all involved were fortunate to have acquired the services of a willing and somewhat experienced organizer—Rose's twenty-year-old brother, Conley Chan. Even while attending college—following in Rose's studious footsteps—the younger sibling had immersed himself in helping plan the weddings of several friends. He had natural organizational abilities, endless energy and an eye for the tweaking and trimming of all of matrimony's ceremonial and decorative trappings.

Conley Chan had assembled the essential participants in the hotel ballroom for the necessary rehearsal. Since he had been drilling the nearly all-Chan party for some time, this last rehearsal would be a mere formality—more for the benefit of the officiating minister and anyone else who had not been put through their paces.

"Where's Henry?" Conley's headcount of groomsmen and bridesmaids had confirmed that only the eldest Chan offspring was absent. Evelyn Chan piped up. "He forgot something—told me he was going back to our room, that he would be right down."

The Statler dining room was prepared for the customary rehearsal dinner, and Conley Chan was keen to keep events on schedule; Henry would have to catch up when he arrived. The wedding party assembled and processed into the ballroom at Conley's direction.

Bride and groom displayed no pre-wedding worries; younger family members were fidgety; elder participants, resigned. The normally jovial Reverend William Pettifather, who surely had presided at more such events than anyone present had attended, seemed nervous. Most of the younger people present took no notice of the rector's fumbling and apparent anxiety, but Charlie Chan missed nothing. Calling to mind the earlier conversation with the man of the cloth at Grace's high tea, he wondered at this strange unease in one so experienced.

"That was perfect—thank you so much," Conley Chan told the group. "Everyone—please remember your place in the procession tomorrow, and bride and groom: don't forget your cues!"

The ballroom was prepared for the event, with a platform for the principal participants and plentiful seating for friends and family. The chairs were grouped in rows left and right, creating a center aisle wide enough for the wedding party to march in stately fashion. As though making up for lost time, Henry Chan now made his way quickly down the aisle—heading toward his father.

"Henry—where were you? We couldn't wait any longer . . . " Conley Chan's chiding trailed off when his grim-faced brother drew closer. Normally dapper in appearance, Henry was a sight: hair tousled, mouth bleeding slightly, suit in disarray.

"Sorry, I was otherwise occupied," the eldest Chan son said wryly. "Dad, we need to talk."

"Perhaps visit to hospital facility in this hotel is in order," Charlie Chan suggested, paternal concern evident in his voice and face. "Medical attention is first priority—talk can wait."

"I'm fine, really I am," Henry insisted. "We need to catch the guy—he was in our suite. I grabbed him, but he slugged me and ran."

"Can you describe unwelcome visitor?" Chan applied his pocket handkerchief to Henry's bloodied face.

"Didn't get a good look at him, worse luck," Henry Chan groaned. "I had just changed my necktie when I heard something, it sounded like someone was trying to spring the lock—to get in. When I jerked the door open, bang! He hit me with his fist, or something very like it. I tried to grab him, but he socked me again, knocked me down. When I got up, he was gone."

"You glimpsed nothing in brief encounter—height? Color of hair?" Charlie Chan looked closely at Henry's face, noting his son's swollen lip and bruised cheek.

Chan's son shook his head and winced. "The hallway's not well lit, and I didn't have time to see much. I'd say he had dark hair and was a bit taller than me, wore a suit—but I couldn't swear as to the color. Sorry, dad."

"No need to apologize—damage to offspring of greater concern, and I am happy that you were not seriously hurt," Charlie Chan said firmly.

He turned to Conley, who was hovering nearby with several concerned siblings. "Please go to nearest telephone and call police headquarters—say that Detective McCaffrey is needed urgently at Hotel Statler."

Conley Chan nodded and left the ballroom, heading for the reception desk.

"Now, then, dear lady—where are you headed?"

The hotel detective, Watkins, was making his rounds on one of the upper floors when he encountered Evelyn Chan's mysterious "lady" making her way down the hall. The woman looked fixedly at Brody Watkins, an expression of uncertainty on her face.

"Do I know you? You seem . . . that is, I think I've seen you before, haven't I?"

Brody Watkins nodded as he gently took her arm. "Sure, sure—we're old friends. I'm Brody Watkins, remember?"

The woman let herself be guided down the hallway

toward the room she had left not long before. As Watkins opened the door for her, she stopped and looked him full in the face.

"Yes—that's right. You're the hotel detective."

Watkins sighed. "Got it in one. Give the lady a cigar."

The woman was puzzled. "Oh—thank you, no. I don't partake, but thank you for seeing me home."

"You're welcome, Mrs.—"

The door closed in the little man's face. Resigned to the situation, he shrugged and continued his rounds.

Mrs. Wilgus paused as the Rector came down the stairs, a valise in his hand. The housekeeper applying a cloth to the banister was a faithful performative duster, so she was glad to see the Reverend Pettifather; more accurately, she was pleased that he had seen her faithfully attending to her duties.

"Ah! Mrs. Wilgus." The clergyman's worried look dissolved into his customary "blessings-upon-you" expression. "I have an appointment—please tell cook that I won't be at home for dinner, thank you."

"Very good, sir." Mrs. Wilgus nodded and returned to her dusting as the door closed behind the man of the cloth. She waited a few seconds, then trundled off toward the kitchen where her comrade-in-arms, Mrs. Gibbons, was hard at work.

"The old boy is off again, Mrs. Gibbons." The stout cook put down a paring knife and looked up quizzically. "Says to tell you he won't be dining in this evening."

"Again? What am I to do with these lamb cutlets, I'd like to know!" Mrs. Gibbons cried in vexation. "For a man in holy orders, he is the most frustrating, infuriating—"

"Yes, yes, all of that, and more," the housekeeper agreed.

"But here, now. Look on the bright side."

The cook applied the knife vigorously to a large white potato; she fancied that it resembled the recently departed Pettifather. "Bright side?"

"Well," the housekeeper replied with a crooked smile. "We're both fond of lamb."

CHAPTER XIV

BRODY WATKINS TRIUMPHANT

Big Mike McCaffrey was beginning to wonder if a solution to the case was slipping out of reach. Frowning in frustration, he lit a cigarette and swallowed some of what passed for coffee at the station house.

Having consumed what he considered the essential fuel for any detective's proper functioning, McCaffrey had begun to mull over recent developments in the investigation when an officer approached.

"Sarge says you're wanted at the Statler," the fresh-faced patrolman announced. "Somebody from the hotel just called, said it was urgent."

Big Mike grabbed coat and hat, wondering what new development could be "urgent." Stopping by the front desk long enough to ask that two officers be dispatched to meet him at the Statler, he exited the station house.

Taxis were not his preferred method of transportation, and this time of day they could be scarce, but he was in luck—an unmarked department vehicle was available. A dozen minutes later, he made his way—quickly—into the hotel lobby, and thence, directed by a bellboy, to the ballroom.

The police detective took in the strange scene with a sweeping glance.

Charlie Chan, his wife and assorted offspring—in short, the wedding party, John Quincy included—were present; Henry, disheveled but recovering, was an item of interest; and Mrs. Winterslip and Miss Minerva, arriving to join the group for dinner and now informed as to recent events, hovered in the background.

The latest additions to this odd conclave were of greater interest to Big Mike. Hotel detective Watkins, his trenchcoat on and a triumphant look on his face, stood guard over a handcuffed and seated Cleveland Armitage, whose normally cinematic appearance was somewhat the worse for wear.

"What goes on here?" McCaffrey demanded of no one in particular. Watkins grinned and nodded at Chan.

"You tell him, Charlie. I want to keep my attention focused on this bird." He patted Armitage on the back in a friendly manner as he prepared his prisoner for a trip to the precinct jail; his prisoner snarled something profane in return.

Chan bowed slightly and summarized recent events for the new arrival.

"Your appearance here is most timely—and helpful," he began. "Son Henry had just reported encounter with heavy-fisted intruder in our rooms, when Mr. Watkins joined us, accompanied by unwilling companion, who has just talked a great deal. I would make suitable introduction, but you will no doubt recall our earlier meeting with Mr. Cleveland Armitage."

"I do, indeed," Big Mike said firmly, "and am I correct in concluding that Mr. Armitage was the man who took a poke or two at you, Henry?"

Henry Chan looked at his father, and at Armitage, then nodded slowly.

"From Chan family suite of rooms, hotel bandit went to next destination," Chan continued. "In that room he no doubt selected items of interest, but while leaving it he made acquaintance of hotel detective."

Although he had planned to let others do the talking, Brody Watkins had collared a thief, and he wanted to make sure he got the credit.

"It was a lovely meeting," Watkins grinned. "He had quite a haul with him, mostly jewelry and cash—I think he's been shopping at the Statler for several days."

The handcuffed Armitage raised his head.

"This place would've been our biggest score ever, if not for the unfortunate fact that—"

"You mean this mug stole the, uh, family item—and then killed the manager?" McCaffrey interrupted the thief and turned to Chan. "Why would he shoot Krednish?"

Charlie Chan returned McCaffrey's puzzled look serenely.

"Recent events at hotel were like tangled string with many knots—crimes were connected, but each was separate. Untying all revealed untangled string in straight line, like truth concealed behind confusion.

"First knot involved three men in criminal enterprise," Chan nodded at Armitage. "One of these three was this very cooperative burglar, who has just—" he looked quizzically at Henry "—spilled the beans?" Henry grinned approvingly at his father's choice of words, and the detective continued.

"At this hotel, two of these three men secured positions; one in management, the other as lowly staff person—elevator operator. Manager would assess targets—wealthy guests, usually—and relay information to third man, who played part of innocent hotel guest. While elevator operator-accomplice assisted and served as lookout, this third man would extract money and valuables from rooms—pretending to be victim himself, when police investigated rash of thefts reported by manager."

Chan paused his story for a moment, turning to Big Mike.

"Suggest you dispatch officer to elevator operator Russum to invite him to police station," he suggested. "His absence from hotel duty suggests he is home or at favorite tavern where we last encountered him."

"I'll take care of it, Charlie," McCaffrey responded, nodding to one of the officers who had just arrived and delivering instructions to him in an undertone.

"Thank you so much," Chan smiled and continued.

"When manager learned of valuable item entrusted to hotel for family event, all three men saw chance to gain large sum by selling it to unworthy 'fence' of stolen items. Fortunately," Chan grinned at the sour-faced captive, "Mr. Armitage thought it better to name Russum than to take sole credit for criminal doings."

"But say!" Watkins objected. "Everybody knew that Gilbert and Krednish had words, that they had worked together before, but you say it was Russum—"

"Pardon interruption, please," Chan interjected. "Krednish had worked with both men previously, and manager deviously let it be known that he and Gilbert had long-running feud. Misdirection concealed his partnership with guilty Russum, for whom Krednish had no great affection."

"Smart on his part," Watkins admitted. "That noisy argument Krednish and Gilbert had, it sure pointed me in the wrong direction."

The hotel detective produced a handkerchief from a breast pocket and wiped his brow.

"So the bottom line is," he continued, "our friend here took the tiara and then got greedy. He shot the manager so he wouldn't have to split the proceeds three ways."

"You are correct as to theft of tiara, but Armitage did not kill unfortunate manager," Charlie Chan told Watkins.

"You did."

CHAPTER XV

"NOT JUST YET"

The room's stunned silence lasted only a few seconds, but it seemed much longer.

Brody Watkins laughed. "Me? Why would I—what possible reason could I have for doing such a thing?"

"Unknown to his accomplices, manager had agreed to keep hidden your wife, so that you could have her close by while you worked to obtain funds enough to secure her future care. In exchange for this arrangement, you allowed thefts from hotel guests to continue without interference. But then, you learned through police department contacts that item of great value would be placed in hotel safe.

"Spending much time in manager's office—and sometimes overhearing private conversations—you discovered Krednish and his associates would steal same—and you threatened manager with exposure and arrest unless he 'cut you in on the deal,' as son Henry would say," Chan told Watkins. "Your share would save troubled wife from uncertain future," Chan told him.

"But when you visited partner in his office to discuss payment, lighting expensive cigar salesman had given you, manager told you of failed plan—family unwilling to pay ransom—and revealed second item of bad news, opinion he obtained from expert: stolen item was worthless.

Maybe you doubted him, suspecting treachery. Regardless of reason, you shot Krednish with his own gun—perhaps grabbing same from cluttered desktop."

Cracks had appeared on the surface of the hotel detective's sunny disposition, and his earlier smile had become more of a grimace. McCaffrey was mystified.

"I don't get it, Charlie," he said. "You sure about this? Watkins did good work at the department, and—"

"Please pardon interruption," Chan said sharply, "but this man kept personal misfortune secret—wife with disease of mind that made her unreliable. He needed first, to keep her safe; and second, to obtain large sum to secure her future."

He turned back to Watkins.

"Manager Krednish was still convinced family would pay sum for return of tiara, and he planned to blame theft on his two partners in previous hotel schemes. First, greed called to him—wealth for one would be greater than dividing same—then, angry moment caused fatal mistake for you—and for Krednish."

"But it wasn't for me," shouted Watkins. "I only wanted to take my Cora away—somewhere warm, someplace where I could take care of her. And I didn't mean to shoot that louse, I just wanted him to hand over my share of the dough and shut his mouth. The gun was just to let him know I meant business—"

"District attorney and perhaps jury will decide fate of man who plots crime and turns on partner in moment of anger," Chan interrupted. "I am happy to relinquish my unofficial role in this case to official authorities."

"Not just yet," Watkins snapped. He had taken a step back, pulling a gun from the pocket of his trench coat. "That's a fine story, Mr. Chan, but you've got the guilty party right here—" he gestured toward Armitage.

"I have an appointment to keep—with my wife," the hotel detective continued, a wild look in his eyes. "Sure, that part of your story is true enough. Not exactly the way you told it, but she was stayin' in a room upstairs while I figured out what to do. And she did wander off some-times—your girl saw her a time or two—but we'll be all right now, she and me, as long as we're together."

He took another step back toward the ballroom exit. "Everybody just stay put," he cried. "It would be a damn shame for this gun to go off and hurt somebody."

As Watkins slowly walked backward, Chan took sev-eral steps forward, coming to a stop in front of him. The advancing detective remained calm, his impassive visage a stark contrast to the retreating man's anguished expression.

"No need to threaten innocent people—with unload-ed gun." Chan held out his hand. "Took liberty of remov-ing bullets from revolver and returning empty weapon to pocket of trench coat where you usually hang same, in lobby cloakroom."

Watkins looked at the gun in his hand, then stared at Chan. The panic and anger in his eyes faded, and the hotel detective slumped in defeat.

"I wasn't going to use it anyway."

He handed over the gun, and McCaffrey nodded to two officers who had been waiting in the doorway. The pair took Watkins and Armitage away, leaving the somewhat puzzled police detective to question Charlie Chan.

"Well, Mr. Chan," McCaffrey began slowly. "I can't say that I followed your reasoning from start to finish, but— well, when did you begin to suspect Brody Watkins?"

The excitement now over, hungry members of the wedding party were making their way to the hotel dining room—the rehearsal dinner had been delayed long enough. Charlie Chan assured his wife, Rose and other family members that he would join them shortly, then turned back to Big Mike.

"Hotel detective arrived unannounced to make introduction, and something told me, 'This man is not as he seems,' but I dismissed that intuition at first—perhaps he was only nervous in manner. Second indication, behavior of manager Krednish and detective Watkins when they called me to examine scene of supposed theft. Both were quick to present conclusions that they wished me to accept—and both spoke like characters in theater who had rehearsed what they would say.

"So, there were some indications early on," McCaffrey said thoughtfully. "I suppose you saw a lot that I didn't when we went over the manager's office—after the body was discovered?"

"We both saw same things—aging detective with suspicious mind drew different conclusions, perhaps," Chan grinned. "In time, with more experience, you will do likewise."

"For one thing, I know that you made a lot more out of that ashtray than I did," Big Mike admitted sheepishly. Chan shrugged.

"No great wisdom was required—and long experience has been great teacher," the detective admitted. "Not many years ago, solution of mystery revealed partly because color-blind man misplaced lids on cigarette boxes. Tobacco use sometimes provide valuable clues."

"To begin, many people coming and going smoked in office. Opportunity to compare contents of ashtray from one day to the next revealed that someone with taste for fine cigar—very expensive—visited manager and sat in chair facing him, as angle of abandoned cigar ash indicated.

"Manager smoked pipe, you extinguished cigarette in ashtray," Chan went on, "but long column of ash from cigar was unique. Had already observed Brody Watkins consuming cigar of inferior type outside of office, but maybe others in hotel had more expensive taste—enlisted housekeeping staff to survey rooms—and questioning of tobacco salesmen revealed that he sometimes offered sample cigarette or cigar to police officers he encountered—"

"And you figured an ex-cop like Watkins probably hit him up for a free cigar," McCaffrey cut in. Chan nodded, grinning, and continued.

"Tobacco expert provided helpful information, and availability of expensive cigar connected one of two hotel guests, this Armitage or Kansas City salesman, to manager's ashtray—perhaps to cigar-smoking hotel detective. Housekeeping search for cigar remnants in room ashtrays" —Chan held up a note from Mrs. Brennan—"revealed same in office of house detective, although she did not recall that he was regular smoker of same. Finding is no surprise, since his habit by itself does not connect him to murder of manager.

"To return to the long and unbroken ash, it indicated man who lights expensive smoking item, but as one unaccustomed to premium brand, leaves maker's band on it to be consumed—cigar expert noted same in analysis of ash—plus distracted smoker allows entire cigar to burn undisturbed in ashtray. I ask myself: What distraction would have caused such forgetfulness?"

"Murder," McCaffrey said grimly. "The visitor was somebody the manager knew, and they were having a friendly chat—and a smoke."

"Such was my first thought, that what started as welcome conversation turned to, perhaps, surprise, anger, disturbance—something that took attention of smoker away from ashtray for several minutes, maybe longer.

"Other indications arose also. Experienced police detective quickly offered theory of visitor who shoots manager from doorway—why? To point away from actual events that he caused, to steer investigation in wrong direction.

"Same for the use of manager's own gun, the leaving behind of same, even suggestion of suicide," Chan continued. "All early signs that former policeman sought to mislead investigators. But why?"

McCaffrey shook his head in disbelief.

"He had a good reputation in the department, and then to land a hotel detective's job with an outfit like the Statler—he seemed to be sittin' pretty," the detective said. "I would never have thought he'd go crooked."

"River that flows over time can change course," Chan observed, "but some would say motive to do wrong was noble—a man's devotion to ailing wife above all else."

The wedding rehearsal dinner atmosphere combined the gaiety of a happy occasion with the celebration of a solved mystery. Guests and staff alike were clearly relieved that recent events no longer overshadowed the impending nuptials, and more than one congratulatory toast was drunk. During the meal lighthearted conversation dominated, but as dessert was served Charlie Chan was much in demand.

"Well, Dad," said Rose, mischievously, "you have much to tell us—don't you?"

"Ask your questions, and I shall do my best to reply to same," her father replied promptly. "Happy to satisfy

curiosity of bride-to-be with same information just supplied to official police, but first"—he surveyed the pie à la
mode that had just arrived in front of him—"must satisfy
appetite for happy ending to celebratory meal."

CHAPTER XVI

A SECOND POT OF TEA

The Winterslip ladies had asked Chan to take early tea with them the morning after the arrest. Even though it was the day of the wedding, the three were mercifully free from obligations until mid-afternoon, as the ceremony itself was to occur at dusk. From the two women's cordial but uneasy demeanor Charlie Chan deduced correctly that this was no mere social occasion.

Miss Minerva Winterslip opened the proceedings.

"Charlie, I want you to know that we—the family—are grateful for bringing this matter to a successful conclusion. Grace and I want the best for John Quincy and Rose, and any hint of scandal now would surely cloud their happiness. That's why we were, and are, anxious to—"

"Anxious to know exactly what you know," Grace broke in.

The detective smiled.

"Happy to enlighten most charming ladies about most elements of recent investigation, now happily concluded—"

"Most?" Miss Minerva put it. "Why not all?"

"I think, perhaps, this lady," Chan gestured toward Mrs. Winterslip, "could solve mystery that has puzzled me—how family that valued tradition so highly could have locked away for many years jewelry that had no value. Reluctance to pay large sum to retrieve heirloom indicated that true value was known."

"Well?" Miss Minerva's alert, birdlike expression turned toward her sister-in-law. "What about it?"

As she usually did, Mrs. Grace Winterslip rose to the occasion.

"It's really quite simple, especially if you had known Mr. Winterslip as I did—not, perhaps, as most people perceived him, but as he really was . . . when he was young—when *we* were young."

Miss Minerva prepared herself for the kind of soliloquy that usually ensued whenever Grace invoked youth and the last decade of the previous century.

"The eighties and nineties, oh—what a time it was! We were the new generation, coming of age at the approach of a new century, there was romance in the very air—"

"I remember," Miss Minerva said softly.

"—and when we learned about the family tradition—the tiara—I'm afraid that we didn't take it seriously. Quite the opposite, in fact."

Mrs. Winterslip was absorbed in the recollection of youthful folly.

"This was at a time when we were, as they say 'just starting out.' I had a bit of a dowry that we anticipated, and Mr. Winterslip was only beginning his career—the family had not settled anything on him at that point.

"The world—the world of finance, at least—was unsettled at the time, too . . . well, I won't go into all the reasons why; suffice it to say that when plans for our happy day were well along, we came into possession of 'the trinket,' as Mr. Winterslip dubbed it, and we decided to . . . "

Miss Minerva sighed. Chan was silent, but one eyebrow

rose slightly.

" . . . Mr. Winterslip took it somewhere—it may have been here, perhaps New York—and engaged the services of a man who must have known his trade, because I couldn't tell the difference between the tiara as it once was, and the tiara that everyone admired on our wedding day.

"The trinket, in fact, that we placed in safekeeping all these years, until—well, the rest you know."

A short silence ensued, broken by Miss Minerva.

"Good heavens, Grace! I don't know what to say, except that curiosity compels me to ask—"

"Yes?"

"What became of the diamonds? The real ones?"

The lady of the house poured herself more tea and offered to do the same for her guests, but both declined. They were more interested in hearing the end of the story.

"Yes, well—a few of them, we sold to the man who did the work. They were, in effect, payment for his creation of what my mother's generation called a 'traveling tiara.' In her time, one didn't want to risk theft of one's precious stones while exposed on long, sometimes dangerous journeys."

She raised a teacup to her lips, and the morning light glinted from rings on her right hand and the choker that encircled her neck. For Charlie Chan, the effect was enlightening.

John Quincy had told the detective of his mother's fondness for jewelry—and her characteristic explanation that no person of their social stratum would flaunt genuine precious stones.

Miss Minerva was impatient.

"A few? What about the rest?"

"Perhaps," Chan interjected, "Noble lady, in her youth, read story by famous American author—tale of hidden letter—"

"Oh, my, no, Mr. Chan," Grace Winterslip twittered. "In my day, girls were guided toward improving books, to be sure, and perhaps a light novel—only to be read sparingly, in the afternoons—but never the kind of sensational fiction to which you refer. At least, I never read such a story.

"However," she paused, a twinkle in her eye. "Mr. Winterslip had."

"Story? What story?" Miss Minerva was mystified.

Chan smiled.

"Secret should be disclosed by lady of refined literary upbringing, not by prying detective's deduction," he pointed out.

"Quite right, Mr. Chan," Mrs. Winterslip replied. "My dear Minerva, please forgive my—reticence? Is that the word I mean? I've had no secrets from you these many years—save this one.

"It seemed to us at the time—young and very nearly giddy as we were then—that poking a rather large hole in a silly old tradition was the thing to do, so we did it, after we were wed and it came into our possession. We didn't tell anyone, of course. Our parents, especially the Winterslips, would have been mortified! My husband simply paid that little man to substitute imitation gems for the real diamonds in the tiara—and to create several items containing the genuine stones that I have worn practically every day since."

"But why? Whatever possessed the two of you to do such a thing?" Miss Minerva cried.

"It wasn't, perhaps, a mature decision," her sister-in-law admitted. "In retrospect, one might even say we were guilty of youthful folly. But, as I've said, we were young and full of opinions.

"The entire family tradition—locking up gems so that they would be seen and admired once in a generation—it seemed rather outdated to us. We wanted to—to, in our own way, reject the past and embrace the future.

"It was, I suppose, petty—even childish, our wish to mock hidebound tradition," she chuckled, "but it seemed at the time a bit of a lark, the idea we came up with, to put the sacred tiara—what was left of it—on daily display. Mr. Winterslip had read a story by Poe—I've forgotten the name—and it gave him the idea that the best place to hide something is—"

"—in plain sight, where everyone can see it," finished Miss Minerva. "*The Purloined Letter*, of course. Oh, Grace—the two of you must have had such a time of it, such fun. A grand joke at the expense of—"

"—no one in particular, we concluded." Mrs. Winterslip smiled. "Our own private joke for many years."

Chan, who had let the family conversation take its natural course, felt his curiosity had been amply satisfied.

"To return to our earlier question, Mr. Chan," Miss Minerva resumed, "we would like very much to know what you may have discovered during your investigations—but didn't tell the police. Or anyone else. We want you to lay your cards on the table. Face up, of course."

The detective's expression was unreadable. He paused for a moment, then broke the awkward silence.

"Old sin casts long shadow," Chan said gently. "But family's long-ago secret was hidden from social judgment for decades—no need for past to arrive in the present now."

Miss Minerva, knowing Chan as she did, was calm, relieved. But Grace Winterslip's eyes widened.

"Secret? What secret? We merely want to know what else you learned, in the course of your investigations, that could cause scandal and worry for those two young—"

"Please." Chan interrupted. "As vulgar American proverb says, removal of feline fur can be accomplished in several ways. Consider—detective who is also father of bride is eager to provide an answer to your question, but single question, like unhappy cat, has many possible answers.

"Perhaps this ancient story would be of interest," he continued. "A king had two daughters, and one son. But his queen died young, and so he sought comfort from a handmaiden in his household. Bad fortune followed, and she died bearing him a second son.

"So, king hid the shame of that far-off time. He could not acknowledge the boy but was determined to see him grow to manhood close at hand. Guilty secret was known to very few, and the boy grew up in his father's castle, but as a servant.

"While the king lived, this young man took on positions of trust. In some ways, he was almost like a member of royal family. This family, they preserved the old king's secret. His rightful son married in due course, and even though one of king's daughters remained unwed," — Miss Minerva smiled at this reference to her unmarried state—"second daughter was of marriageable age. Her prospects were many."

"You're quite a good storyteller, Mr. Chan," Minerva Winterslip interjected. "I suppose you know what happened to my sis—I mean to say, to the other daughter?"

"Ah! King had high hopes for this princess. Perhaps she would choose wisely and join his royal line to some other family of noble blood," Chan went on. "But she had always been a free spirit, the princess—not like her brother, who married well, or even her half-brother, who accepted humble place in the world.

"She would have her own way, and in the end she married an unsuitable person. The king was furious, and it was given out that she had gone away, far away. It was even hinted that she had died in some distant land, even though she lived, as a commoner, not far from the family that no longer acknowledged her.

"In fairy tale, happy ending often happens." Chan's voice softened perceptibly. "Not so in this case. Even as a young woman, this princess was different in some way. It was plain for all to see that her mind was troubled, in small ways at first, but this affliction was made worse by age, and by the death of her unsuitable husband. She married again, to another commoner, and became more and more . . . unpredictable. Her second husband . . . he did what he could to make her well, keep her safe—"

"I'm sure that the family tried their best to help," Miss Minerva said thoughtfully. "Perhaps small sums discreetly delivered provided some support, but what could they do? Her husband is a proud man . . ."

Chan nodded.

"Family rejection many years ago was deeply felt and cast long shadow. Now, woman's proud husband will be called to account for his misdeeds. Even though his only wish was to protect and care for the one he loved."

The detective hesitated briefly, not wishing to pry.

"What becomes of this troubled woman, Cora? Without loyal husband, what will happen to her?"

Before Miss Minerva could reply, Grace Winterslip answered with one of her brief flashes of common sense.

"It's comforting to me that you don't know, and haven't discovered, everything, Mr. Chan. I was beginning to think that you were clairvoyant! As to that, how on earth did you come to—that is, where did you get the information for this—this story?"

"Many years spent seeking hidden truths in public documents have been most useful training for detective work," Chan admitted. "In this case, it was not hard to assemble family tale from examination of records. Earlier viewing of ancestral portraits in this house had suggested resemblance to more recent person—even under painted whiskers of bygone era."

"Well! While I enjoyed your fable very much, I want to assure you that—in the real world we occupy—an old wrong has been addressed. Not undone, of course, because that would be impossible. But Cora is receiving the best possible care. She has been since the arrest of her husband—that's when Minerva and I became more fully aware of how her condition had worsened."

Miss Minerva nodded, her eyes dimming.

"Grace and I are going to make sure that whatever can be done, will be done. And, when the time is right, we hope to introduce John Quincy and Rose to a long-lost member of the family."

"Kindness today can atone for unfortunate yesterday," Chan replied. "Please pardon this last intrusion on family privacy—what of the second son?"

Mrs. Winterslip sighed.

"I have always maintained a façade of sorts, a pretense—treating him as someone, well, 'almost like a member of the family,' as people say. We have never spoken of his actual antecedents, but whatever he may have said or done—"

"He's a Winterslip," Miss Minerva said tartly. "I took the liberty of speaking to him recently, in complete confidence, of course, and he quite candidly admitted that he has long known all that there is to know about—his heritage, everything. He and Mr. Watkins developed a kind of friendship, more of an alliance, I would say. They spoke regularly, I believe, mostly about mundane things—Cora, the impending wedding, other happenings at the hotel and here in this house."

Chan nodded.

"No doubt their talk of wedding plans included gossip about valuable item required for ceremony, and thus the close connection between servant in household and hotel detective had unfortunate consequences."

"I don't think he fully realized what Brody Watkins and the others had planned at the hotel," Miss Minerva reflected. "He regrets the death of the manager, but he doesn't feel responsible."

"Why should he?" Grace Winterslip interjected. "What Mr. Watkins did—for those things, he should be held accountable. 'Let justice run down like'—something. And righteousness, too. If only the Rector were here, I'm sure he could remember the complete quotation."

Miss Minerva sidestepped the scriptural reference. "At any rate, Mr. Chan, the king's second son your parable described—he is a faithful retainer and will remain so."

"Yes, indeed," Grace Winterslip replied. "So many old families we know—I've often heard them remark that an old servant is 'just like a member of the family.' In this household, that is no idle boast."

As if on cue, Greynebin entered the parlor depositing a second pot of tea and removing the empty one.

"May I bring you and your guests anything else, ma'am?" The gray-haired butler awaited instructions.

"I think not, Greynebin, but thank you, and—" Grace Winterslip hesitated.

"Yes, ma'am?"

The family matriarch reconsidered.

"Nothing further, I think. Just—thank you."

"Very good, ma'am. Miss Minerva, Mr. Chan." He nodded to each in turn.

The faithful Greynebin departed, bearing all the family's secrets, and an empty teapot.

CHAPTER XVII

THE SILVER-HAIRED MAN

At the Statler, the day began with all the last-minute hustle and bustle of a wedding day.

Still, so much had happened in the days preceding it that members of the wedding party suffered none of the usual prenuptial jitters. The bride was excited, happy that no side issues remained to cloud the occasion.

After a final day of anticipation, eventide had arrived. The ceremony was at hand.

Chans were everywhere. Inside the ballroom, the Chan Kim Lee family was among the expectant guests; the bride's mother, Chan Chun Shee, had already been seated by her son William, one of several Chan ushers. The all-Chan bridal party was gathered in a private lounge near the hotel ballroom, awaiting its cue to process into the ceremony from Conley Chan.

A knock at the door silenced the several conversations in the bridal party waiting room, and the younger siblings took their place in line expectantly. Henry Chan opened the door.

The Winterslip "sisters" entered the room, and Miss Minerva, her expression grim, closed the door behind them. Mrs. Grace Winterslip looked troubled; she grasped Rose's hands as Charlie Chan looked on.

"My dear, we are the bearers of bad tidings, I'm sorry to say. Much as it saddens me to darken what should be the happiest—"

"The minister, the esteemed Rector Pettifather, has absconded," Miss Minerva cut in. "Flown the coop. Made tracks. Skedaddled, blast him, and probably not empty-handed."

"Gone?" Rose cried. "But—but—"

"My sentiments exactly," Grace Winterslip said gently, grasping both of Rose's hands. "Most unexpected. Terribly inconvenient, as well."

"Inconvenient is hardly the word for it," Miss Minerva fumed. "Criminal is the word that comes to mind."

Rose had blanched. "The ceremony—we've got to get him back!"

"Well . . . the chances of that happening are, I must say, at best—not that I view a circumstance of this kind as a matter for speculation or wagering, but—"

Mrs. Winterslip's soliloquy was cut short.

"Retrieving the missing rector wouldn't meet your impending need to solemnize the exchange of vows, my dear," Miss Minerva said impatiently, growing weary of her sister-in-law's dithering. "I'm afraid we'll have to look elsewhere."

"I don't understand!" Rose was in tears. "What do you mean?"

"The man was a fraud," Miss Minerva said firmly. "He wasn't a minister at all, but a very experienced confidence man. A New York insurance detective has been making inquiries, and this Pettifather—or whatever his real name is—must've realized that it was time to move on. The police have been notified, since it appears that some of the church's funds departed with him."

Rose was distraught; how could she and John Quincy

have a wedding without a clergyman? She directed a look of appeal toward her father, who remained outwardly calm. Even the Winterslip "sisters" were at a loss, since neither wealth nor social position could produce a man of the cloth at a moment's notice.

"Perhaps I might be of some assistance?"

A silver-haired man of erect bearing and courtly manner had opened the door and stood framed in the doorway. Just behind this new arrival, John Quincy was attempting to navigate a path between his conflicting roles: a groom who must not see his bride in full regalia until the ceremony and an interested participant in the unfolding events. He could see few of the bridal party members in the room but noticed that Aunt Minerva was blushing, apparently at the site of the distinguished newcomer. Without looking further at the wedding party, the groom hastily performed introductions through the half-open door.

"Mother, may I present Captain Arthur Cope, of the British Navy—the Admiralty, most recently—"

"Happily retired from my duties, I must add," Cope added. "Mrs. Winterslip, a pleasure."

"My fiancé, Rose Chan, and her father, whom you met some years ago," John Quincy's voice continued. " . . . and I believe you know this lady?"

Cope smiled.

"Indeed I do. Miss Winterslip—I must apologize for turning up at such irregular intervals, twice in Hawaii and now here."

"'Miss Winterslip'—fiddlesticks! Arthur Cope, you must be the most persistent—"

The former captain cleared his throat.

"I would be quite pleased to go into that subject with you, at some length, later. At the moment, or so I've been informed, these two young people are in need of some assistance."

Miss Minerva, recovered from the shock of seeing Arthur Cope again after so many years, took charge.

"I'm sure we're all very grateful for your concern, but this is a family matter—and what, may I ask, do you propose to do—that is, how do you know anything about it?"

"I told him." The groom was just outside the lounge, but he could still take part in the council of war. "Hang it all, Captain Cope is the answer to a prayer in the current situation."

"What Mr. Winterslip means to say," Cope offered modestly, "is that I can officiate—and would be happy to do so."

"Bosh." Miss Minerva was having none of it. "I knew a lawyer once who said captains of ships having the power to marry people was an old wives' tale.

"Besides," she continued, "you're retired and are no longer captain of—"

"True enough," Cope admitted. "However, I wasn't always at sea, you know. In my youth I was a theology student, here in Boston, after coming across from England, and I pursued my studies to the point of—"

"No return?" Grace Winterslip felt the need to contribute; she had been silent far too long.

"—ordination. I had occasion to officiate at a cousin's wedding ceremony a few weeks ago, so I took the precaution of consulting church and government authorities. It seems," Cope concluded, "that I am still capable of . . ."

"As I always say, 'Once a parson, always a parson,'" the invisible John Quincy chimed in from the hallway. "Shall I have them strike up the band?"

THE END

ABOUT THE AUTHOR

John L. Swann has worked as a broadcast journalist and in public relations and marketing. His career has included stints as a television news director and anchor and a radio anchor, reporter and talk show host. After leaving broadcasting, he served as chief of staff to the president of the State University of New York Institute of Technology where he authored *From the Mills to Marcy*, a history of the college. A native of the rural Midwest, he lives in Upstate New York with his wife, Patricia, whose years of encouragement were the impetus for the writing of *Death, I Said*, the first in a series of new Charlie Chan mysteries that continues with *The Tangled String*.